EMBRACING LOVE BEYOND DEATH

AVA WIXX

WICKED Press WIXX

Embracing Love Beyond Death

First Edition: March 2024
Published in the United States of America by
Wicked Wixx Press.
The Wicked Wixx Press Logo is a trademark of
Wicked Wixx Press.
Originally published under the title
Embracing Death: May 2013

Cover Art, Ava Wixx Logo, Wicked Wixx Logo, & Interior Book Graphics by Lindsay Tiry of LT Arts
Edited by Melissa Ringsted of There For You Editing

Print ISBN: 978-1-955950-30-5
Kindle ISBN: 978-1-955950-31-2
EPUB ISBN: 978-1-955950-32-9

For more information visit: avawixx.com

Content Warning

Dear Readers,

The characters in this three-book series are extremely flawed, which translates to a ton of questionable behavior. In other words, if you're not a fan of morally grey MCs who fuck up a lot, then you might not want to read this series.

And on that note, if swear words bother you, then this series might not be for you. (Personally, I don't think there are a lot of F-bombs or anything like that, but I cuss so much that I don't notice anymore. Although I do keep the language cleaner when I'm writing … it's easier to spot on page. *shrugs*)

Basically, this is not a light and fluffy story, but rather a dark romance. Although in comparison to what's out there nowadays it's more dark-ish than anything.

Like I mentioned in *Feeling Love Beyond Death's* warning, this series gets darker as it goes along, and

Embracing Love Beyond Death has a bit more of the death addiction intermingled with sex going on. I feel it's a natural progression within the storyline, but if the first book was more than you could handle, I'd recommend not continuing the series.

Now that we have all of that out of the way, if you've decided to proceed ... Happy reading!

~Ava

For those of you who aren't afraid to sit in the dark.

DEATH IS THE
ULTIMATE ADDICTION...

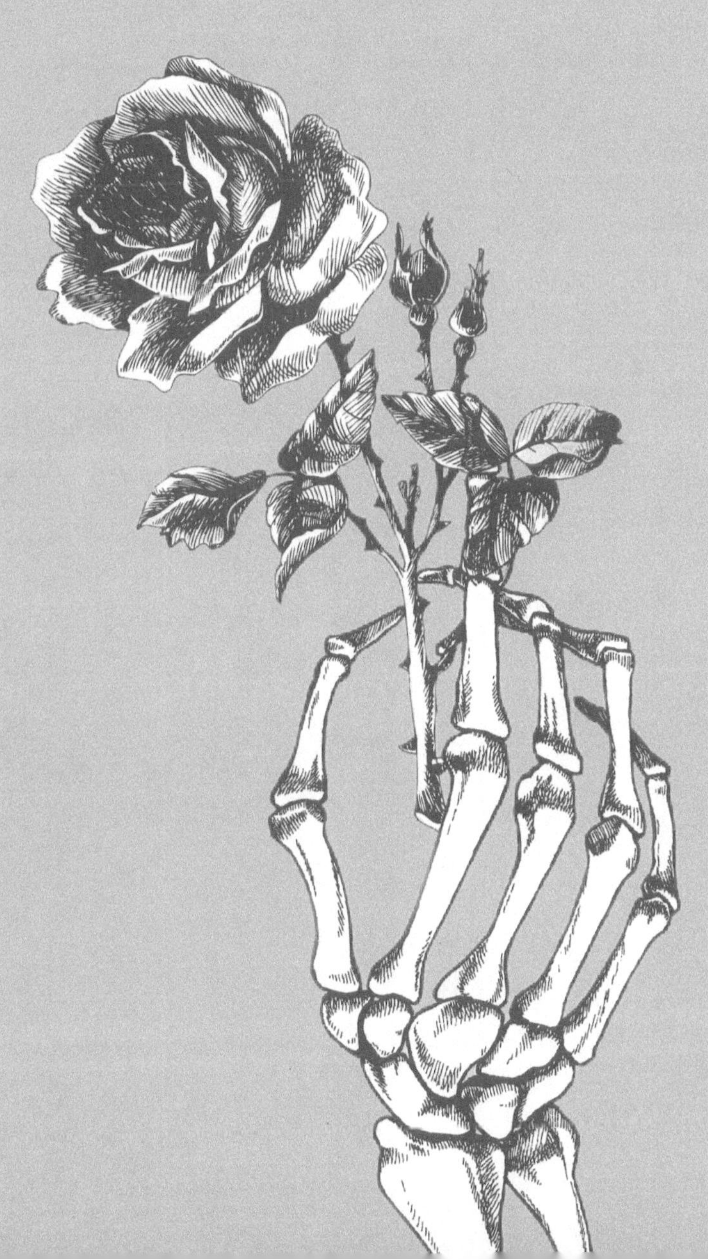

Prologue

If you sit in the dark long enough, your eyes will adjust.

If you completely immerse yourself in death, eventually it will welcome you home into its sweet embrace.

Chapter 1

The thready pulse beat its staccato rhythm against my temples, tapping its way into my mind and ricocheting around my skull. The raspy inhale and exhale of breath wound itself inside my ears like a familiar yet morbid song. The tang of copper filled my nose and exploded on my tongue.

She was dying. I could *feel* it … quite literally.

And the high it gave me, her last moments on this plane of existence … it was a thing of beauty, and I was reveling in it.

"Sam, no!" Austin's deep voice echoed somewhere in the distance.

"So much regret and pain," I mumbled. "I need to feel it until the end. I need to—"

I blinked back tears as the connection was yanked away from me. "No!" I gasped. "I need back in!" I was flustered, confused, and completely alone in my mind. No more glorious feelings of death. "I'm going to miss it! I'm going—"

"You're not missing anything, Sam. She's going to live. They're going to save her." Austin gripped my shoulders tightly, his fathomless eyes holding me captive. "Snap out of it before anyone notices," he grated between clenched teeth. "Sam, please."

Realization hit me, and tears spilled down my cheeks. I wanted her to die, and I wanted to feel it. I should have been ashamed of myself, and yet I wasn't. "Austin," I croaked, letting my eyes slide shut so I didn't have to look at him anymore.

He cupped my head, pulling me against his chest. Shuddering with relief, I inhaled his spicy scent. Austin was my safe harbor, and no matter what happened, being surrounded by him gave me comfort.

"I've got you, Sam. You know I always will. Let's get you out of here." He dropped his voice, whispering, "I'll think up an excuse later."

I nodded my acquiescence, and let Austin lead me away from the crime scene. The red and blue lights danced off the pavement, causing a dreamlike ambiance to wash over me. Or maybe a better description would be nightmare because that's exactly what my life had become.

Chapter 2

"Breathe in his last breath, knowing that your chest will continue to rise and fall. Feel his heartbeat for the last time, even as yours speeds up with excitement. Taste his remorse—his regret for all the things he's leaving behind. Feel his death completely, knowing you'll go on and he will cease to be. Drink down the bitter ambrosia of knowing death, yet not in the true sense of it. Feel it with me, Sam, and grow to love it like I do."

My eyes snapped open, the memory of Malcolm's voice lingering in my mind. I was disoriented for a moment until Austin grumbled something in his sleep, then pulled me more firmly against his chest. The warmth of his hard body seeped into my back, making me want to wrap him around me to chase away the chill of my dark thoughts completely.

Malcolm might be dead, but he was still very much

with me. Every time I closed my eyes he was there, reminding me of the addiction he'd opened up inside of me. *Death*. I longed to taste it again. Which was why Austin had shut me off from my empath abilities. He was convinced if I 'detoxed' then I'd be able to stay clean, like my addiction was some kind of tangible substance or drug. What neither one of us wanted to admit was that it was probably too late for his efforts. But I'd always excelled at denial … and now was no exception.

"Sam, my Sammy girl." Austin's soft, firm lips pressed against the back of my neck. "Are you having trouble sleeping again? Did you have another nightmare?"

I grimaced, glad he couldn't see my face. "I don't want to talk about it."

Suddenly, I found myself on my back, Austin's azure gaze piercing mine with scrutiny. "We don't hide things, especially things like that, from each other."

Entwining my fingers in his sleep-mussed hair, I met his gaze steadily. "I'm not hiding it from you … I just don't want to talk about it."

"Talking about it will help. If you—"

"Talking is overrated," I purred, tugging Austin's face down to meet mine.

He groaned as I aggressively laid siege to his mouth. Letting my hands slide down the smooth expanse of his back, I possessively clutched the muscled orbs of his ass. I pulled him to me, wrapping my legs around his waist to position him right where I wanted.

"Have I mentioned how much I love it when we sleep naked?" Austin murmured against my lips.

He plunged into me, building a slow and steady rhythm, which had me arching in ecstasy in no time. I dug my heels into his lower back to urge him to go faster—harder. I wanted to be owned by him, branded.

Sensing my need, Austin gladly complied, and unintelligible things spilled from my mouth as he pounded into me. I scaled my nails down his back, liking the way it spurred Austin on to take me with an almost desperation. I hurtled over the edge of another release, my senses reveling only in what Austin was making me feel. It was just him and me, and in that moment, I believed our love could fix everything—I believed it would be enough.

"Fuck," Austin muttered, pulsing his own release into me. He dipped his head to nibble my ear lobe. "I love you, Sam. We'll make it through this. I just got you back, I won't lose you again."

I remained silent, not wanting to break our intimacy. I simply trailed my hands over his slightly damp skin, letting them speak for me. They told him I wanted to believe him, that I loved him, and that I hoped what he said was true.

"Talk to me, Sam. Tell me what you're thinking."

"I wish I didn't have to." I heaved a huge sigh and started making small circles on Austin's shoulders with my fingertips. "I miss you being able to just slip into my mind."

Austin chuckled. “As I recall, you always hated it when I slipped into your mind. You complained about it being a breach of privacy.”

I smiled sheepishly. “Well, now that you’ve cut me off completely, I miss you always poking around in my thoughts. It made me feel close to you.”

Austin stilled, his warm breath tickling my neck. “And you don’t feel close to me now?” He pushed himself up on his arms so he could meet my gaze. “How much closer to me could you feel? I’m still inside of you, Sam.”

As if to illustrate his point, Austin rotated his pelvis, and I felt him surge back to life. I moaned at the delicious friction.

“I suppose maybe I just needed reminding of that fact.” I bit into Austin’s shoulder as he continued his slow assault on my body. He then pushed my arms up over my head to restrain me.

“I’ll be happy to remind you as often as you need.” Austin’s lips slammed into mine, his tongue delving into my mouth.

I relished the taste of him, never wanting to let it go. I wanted to drown in his essence so nothing dark could ever touch me again. And for the moment, that’s exactly what I did. I let Austin wash me away in a sea of pleasure.

"DAMNIT!" I muttered, eyeing the target—the target I kept missing. Not completely, but I was nowhere near my normal accuracy. I was too distracted.

After setting the 9mm handgun down, I tore off my protective eye gear and stomped out of the gun range. It'd only been a few weeks since Austin and Taryn's daring rescue to get me from Malcolm's clutches, but I was more than ready to put everything behind me. At first, I was surprised at how accepting Natalie had been of my desire to return to the team. Then again, I wasn't one to look a gift horse in the mouth. I was back, and all of my memories had sorted themselves out.

My biggest issue was dealing with my forced betrayal of Austin. And because I'd been living with Nixon as my husband, I couldn't bring myself to ask the one question I really wanted to of Austin: Had he slept with anyone in the years he thought I was dead? I knew I wouldn't have any right to be angry. I was the first and only girl Austin had ever loved.

I understood that if he fucked someone it would have been just that—fucking. There wouldn't have been real emotions attached to the act. It would never compare to what we had and do share. I'd at least gotten over my insecurities to realize that much.

Yet I still couldn't help but wonder. Every girl Austin was even the tiniest bit friendly with, I found myself studying his reactions, wanting to see if I could suss out the information without having to ask for it.

Case in point. I internally huffed. Rounding the corner

to head back to our room, I spotted Austin in the middle of the hallway talking to a pretty blonde. As I neared them, her hand reached up to make contact with his arm, causing me to grind my teeth.

Austin always was and always would be an enormous flirt. I was okay with it … really. He never did it in a concerning way, and even now I wasn't worried about him cheating on me. No, I was contemplating what the chances were that something happened between him and the blonde while Austin thought I was dead. Had he tried to bury his pain—in her?

Jealousy burned through me, making it difficult to breathe. Narrowing my eyes at the blonde Austin was chatting up, I slid my arms around his waist possessively.

Without hesitation, Austin pulled me tighter into his side and kissed the top of my head. "Hi," he murmured.

"Hi," I responded, while still giving the blonde my full scrutiny. She was short, curvy, and exuded a peppy vibe that made me want to throttle her.

Stop. You're being petty and mean. Even if she did sleep with Austin, it wouldn't be her fault. He thought you were dead.

"Tasha, this is my wife, Sam. Sam, Tasha." Austin's fingers tightened on my hip in a silent request for me to play nice.

"Hey," I said noncommittally.

"Nice to meet you, Sam. I've heard so much about you." Tasha gave me a forced smile.

For the millionth time, I wished I could use my empath abilities to read someone. Was Tasha nervous because she wanted Austin, or did she already have him and was now facing down his not-so-dearly-departed wife? Or maybe my attitude was a bit intimidating? *Damn, I can't wait until I have use of my abilities again.*

When I didn't say anything else, Tasha shifted uncomfortably, glancing over her shoulder. "Oh, well, I'll see you guys around then. Bye, Austin … bye, Sam." Tasha's voice wavered with uncertainty as she said my name.

I smirked as she turned and fled down the hallway.

Austin chuckled. "Jealous much?"

"Yeah, well …" I couldn't think of anything to defend myself, and I knew there was no point in denying it either.

Austin's eyes twinkled. "It's okay, Sam. I kind of like it when you get this way. It shows you still care."

I quirked my eyebrow. "Really? As if there was any doubt?"

Austin skimmed his nose up my jawline towards my earlobe, which he caught gently between his teeth. I shivered with delight. "Well, you know …" His breath tickled my ear and goose bumps erupted across my flesh. "I have such low self-esteem you're going to have to constantly reassure me how much you want me, my good little Sammy girl."

I rolled my eyes. "Yes, you have the lowest self-esteem of anyone I know, clearly."

"I do. Good thing my wife doesn't seem to mind the kind of reassurance I need." He dipped his head to whisper in my ear, "Let's go back to our room. I could use some of your brand of—"

Austin's body tensed around mine. "What the hell are you doing here?"

I swiveled around in Austin's arms, gasping when my gaze met familiar brown eyes. "Nixon," I croaked.

What the fuck?

Chapter 3

Shock surged through my system, paralyzing me. I hadn't seen Nixon since the night I'd been reunited with Austin. Taryn had forcefully removed him from the hotel room, and I'd just assumed he wouldn't be darkening my doorstep any time soon—if at all.

Nixon's lips pulled back in a sneer as he locked gazes with me. "What? You think you're the only one that Natalie would be so forgiving of? At least I didn't help kill anyone … and enjoy it."

"How dare you!" Rushing him, I managed to connect my open palm with his face. The satisfying sting against my flesh spurred me to do it again … and again. With each recoil I swung, no intention of stopping.

Austin yanked me away, moving us both a few steps back.

Nixon smirked despite the inflamed skin along his

jawline and cheek. "I know you enjoy inflicting pain on other people, so should I consider this foreplay? Do you miss me, Sam?"

I stilled, my emotions rolling through anger, confusion, and finally settling on sadness. Nixon may not have been my husband all those years, but I thought he was. I'd trusted him, and he'd betrayed me. On top of everything else, now he seemed to want to antagonize me.

"Why?" I whispered.

Pain and regret filled Nixon's eyes, darkening their chocolate color. "You're my wife. How do you think it makes me feel to see you with him now?"

Fresh shock shot through my system, and I eyed him incredulously. "I was never your wife. It was all a lie."

Nixon's jaw muscles ticked. "You can't tell me what you felt for me wasn't real. All those times we were together …" He slammed his fist into the wall beside him. "I was inside you, Sam. In your heart, too. I know I was."

I shook my head. If he hadn't essentially abducted and brainwashed me, then maybe I would feel sorry for him. As it was, my emotions towards him were a snarled, tangled mess best left untouched. "Lies. All lies. What you thought I felt for you was all for Austin. It's always been him. You know that, Nixon. Stop lying to yourself."

"He's ruined you!" Nixon roared, his face reddening. "I tried to protect you! I gave you a life where you could do what you wanted—help people, but without the darkness!"

Austin barked out a humorless laugh. "You betrayed

me, Nixon. You were my best friend, and you stole my wife. You're lucky I don't kill you. It would be worth any repercussions it brings my way."

"You can *try* to kill me. Try. Go ahead, *friend*." Nixon's chest heaved. "And don't forget who had her first. You stole her from me, I simply took her back."

"You don't love *me*." My voice was cold and hard. "You love who you want me to be. But Austin loves who I actually am. And let me also remind you that I'm not a possession to be taken. I choose who I'm with. Not you, and not Austin."

Nixon loved someone who didn't exist. He was convinced that Austin ruined me, but in reality, Austin made me want to be a better person because he accepted every part of me—even the darkest pieces.

Nixon's whole body seemed to deflate. "That's not true," he rasped. "I know who you are, and I love you."

"Enough," Austin growled. "We could go back and forth like this all day." He took my hand within his and intertwined our fingers. "Come on." He tugged me after him as he started in the opposite direction.

"What?" I said with surprise. "You're just going to walk away? After—"

"He was a friend once. And even though I want to kill him," Austin's hand tightened almost painfully around mine, "I know he did what he did out of love."

"More like obsession," I grumbled.

"Yeah, but isn't any kind of true love about obsession, just a little bit anyways? I know I'm obsessed with you."

Austin's words gave me pause. I slowly mulled them over. Hadn't I been obsessed with Austin, just a little? Even in the beginning, when I didn't want to desire him, I knew the answer was still yes. And Austin just admitted he was obsessed with me.

I sighed. "Point taken."

"Yeah, well, I'm always right." He smirked.

I shook my head ruefully. "I love you, but I'm never going to stop wishing you'd tone down your ego a bit."

Austin let go of my hand and wrapped his arm around my waist, smiling down at me. "Then I wouldn't be who I am, and you wouldn't love me anymore."

My mood sobered as I gazed into his eyes. "I'll always love you. I loved you even when I didn't remember who you were."

His smile melted, and I suddenly found his mouth slanted over mine, his tongue pushing past my lips aggressively. I grasped his shirt and hooked my leg over his hip, rocking into him.

"I was wondering if the two of you might have forgotten where you were?"

I pulled away from Austin, my cheeks heating. Natalie stood at the end of the hallway, wearing an amused expression. Her short, silver hair seemed to glow in the harsh neon lighting. I carefully kept my mouth shut so I wouldn't blurt out something inappropriate, like I wished she would go away immediately. Natalie's gift of forcing people to be one hundred percent truthful around her was a curse for everyone besides her.

"I would say I'm sorry, Natalie, but I can't, as you know." Austin grinned, completely unrepentant.

"You wouldn't say you're sorry even without Natalie's truth-whammy ability," I snarked.

"True." Austin's grin made me want to start kissing him again.

"All right. Well, now that I've found you two, if you would both accompany me back to my office so that we can have the meeting that I sent Austin to retrieve you for." Natalie turned on her high heels, obviously expecting us to follow.

I slapped Austin's arm with annoyance. "Really? She sent you to come get me, and you were going to mention that when?"

He shrugged. "We got a bit distracted."

"Ummm … yes we did, but I found you, remember? Chatting it up with that stupid blonde girl outside of the gun range."

Guess he'd gotten distracted twice. I gritted my teeth, fighting unfounded jealousy. Austin was mine, and whatever happened while he thought I was dead didn't matter. Even still, when Austin reached for my hand, I shirked away from him.

"Aw, come on, Sam. Really?"

"After we meet with Natalie we need to talk." I knew it wouldn't matter in the long run, but I just had to know. Maybe if I knew then I could move past any indiscretions he might have had. After all, wasn't knowledge supposed to be power?

"I don't think I like the sound of that," Austin mumbled.

"Don't worry, it will only be painful for me." I gulped down the sour taste in my mouth, focusing on the task at hand—our meeting with Natalie. I would deal with my insecurities afterward. Hopefully, my fears would turn out to be unfounded.

I glanced over at Austin, running my gaze over his thick, nearly black hair and sculpted profile, then down his muscular body. *Yeah right, who am I kidding*? He thought I was dead, and who wouldn't jump at the chance to try and comfort Austin with their body?

I better prepare myself for one tough conversation.

Chapter 4

"Nixon's back," Natalie stated as soon as Austin and I entered her office.

"Yeah, we're aware," Austin snapped.

Natalie scowled. "I'm guessing that's because he didn't obey my orders to stay away from the two of you, at least until I had the chance to talk to you both first."

"Ummm ... nope. He's already skulking around, waiting to antagonize us whenever possible." Yep, my filter was fully off because of Natalie, and I hated it, as usual.

Ignoring me, Austin offered his own take on the matter. "He seems very bitter and angry about Sam and me being together. Why did you let him come back here?"

Natalie raised her eyebrows in surprise. "Do you think my forgiveness is limited to the two of you? What we do here serves a higher purpose—"

Austin slammed his fist into Natalie's desk. "Damn it!

He abducted my wife! And he had her brainwashed into think she was married to him! He fucking hijacked both of our lives!"

I grabbed Austin's hand, inspecting it for any damage, finding none. "We killed people, Austin. We killed people that didn't deserve to die. You killed Jessica, and I killed all those people with Malcolm, and Natalie brought us back. What Nixon did, by comparison—"

Austin swung his head around to look at me, his eyes widening. "Are you seriously going to defend him right now?" He snatched his hand out of my grasp.

"No. It's just that I understand where Natalie is coming from, Austin. We're lucky she's so forgiving, and we can't expect her to make us the exceptions."

Austin glowered, his gaze fixated on the floor.

"Nixon loves you, Samantha," Natalie stated.

Austin exploded from his chair, his face flushed with fresh anger. "Why the fuck would you say that to her? To us? What kind of shit are you trying to pull?"

He paced across the room, mumbling to himself, "I know how you're always trying to mess with people's lives —shaping and controlling. I've seen it. You can't tell me you didn't have any clue about Sam and Nixon and what happened to them. But why would you keep it a secret? Why ... why ... why?"

I wasn't sure if Austin realized what he was saying out loud since his words seemed like inner musings. Regardless, it sounded like he was accusing Natalie of knowing what Nixon had done from the beginning. I rose slowly, and hesitantly placed myself in Austin's path.

"What are you saying?" I bit my lower lip, meeting his intense gaze with question.

Instead of answering, Austin swung around towards Natalie. "Well, did you? Did you know Sam was still alive and that Nixon had her?"

Natalie met his gaze steadily. "I had my suspicions. The fact that Nixon disappeared without a trace was my first clue, but whoever was hiding them—and when I say whoever I mean someone was cloaking them—whoever was doing that was extremely talented." She sighed heavily. "What good would it have done to tell you what I suspected when you couldn't have done anything about it?"

"If we were cloaked, then how did you find me, Austin?"

"Jessica," he hissed, as if her name answered everything.

And maybe it did. Austin killed her, not on purpose, but because he'd been enraged to the point where his abilities had spun out of control. The catalyst had been learning that she helped Nixon with his plan and then kept it a secret.

Austin pulled me into his arms, tucking my head under his chin. "Once I knew you were alive, there was nothing that could have kept me from finding you. Nothing."

We stood in utter silence for a handful of Austin's heartbeats before Natalie cleared her throat. "This isn't why I wanted to talk with you two. I mean yes, I wanted to let you know about Nixon's return, but there are more important things we need to discuss."

I turned my head towards Natalie while still within Austin's embrace. "Yeah, like what?"

It was then it struck me that I had no idea who Natalie really was, or who funded her little operation. I'd always been under the impression that we were some kind of secret task force that the government funded. But Malcolm had clued me in to that being a falsehood. Nixon and I had been working for the government—so was what he told me true? Was the group that Natalie was in charge of really run by some do-gooder with too much money on their hands? Did it really matter since Natalie's team seemed like the good guys? How could I have my memories back and yet still have so many unanswered questions?

"For one," Natalie nodded at me, "we need to discuss your little problem."

"I'm handling it," Austin growled.

Natalie raised her eyebrows at Austin. "Shutting off her abilities isn't solving anything. You're merely helping Samantha avoid her problems, not cope with them."

I pulled away from Austin, slumping back into my chair. "What do you suggest then?"

"I suggest letting things work themselves out naturally."

"What?" Austin's jaw muscles feathered as he fought to stay still.

I grabbed his hand, preventing him from hitting anything again.

"You can't be serious," I said absently, my attention focused on Austin who was practically vibrating with hostility. I tightened my grip on him, hoping there weren't any more impending physical outbursts. His nerves were frayed, which was making his temper short. And I couldn't help but blame myself for all of it.

"I'm not going to let her become like Malcolm," Austin grated. "Because I won't let you have her eliminated. You know I'd kill for her if I have to."

"It won't come to that," Natalie assured us. "What we need is a plan of action, and I have exactly that."

I was at least willing to listen. After all, what did I have to lose—besides everything?

"I DON'T KNOW about all of this," I muttered under my breath, staring out the window of Natalie's private jet. The dark sky beyond the glass seemed to be a reflection of my mood, worry and anxiety mingling in my gut.

We were currently on our way to the scene of an apparent terrorist attack—a bombing. There would be dozens of dead bodies for me to pick up on their dying emotions for clues. That's where Austin and my abilities differed slightly. He couldn't pick up on the recently dead's emotions in the same manner that I could. In other words, death was my specialty. His talents lay more with manipulation of emotions and memory. And although what Natalie said made sense—I couldn't avoid my issues, I had to confront them head-on—I couldn't help feeling it was all a huge mistake.

"You okay?" Austin punctuated his inquiry with a squeeze of my hand.

I nodded without looking away from the window.

Austin's hand cupped the side of my face, turning me towards him. His azure eyes ensnared me in their fathomless depths as he spoke, "We'll make it through this."

I gnawed on my bottom lip. "What if I do become like him?" I didn't need to clarify who *him* was —Malcolm.

Austin's thumb stroked my cheek gently. "You won't. I won't let that happen, I promise."

"You can't make that promise. No one can." Austin opened his mouth to protest, but I didn't want to delve into my issues with death again. Instead, I opted to do a quick subject change. "We still need to talk about some things." A subject change, yes, but not exactly a less difficult matter to discuss. I paused to study Austin's expression.

Am I being an idiot by bringing this up? Probably ... but I have to know.

"Spit it out, Sam. I can practically see the wheels turning in your head."

"Yeah, okay." Sighing, I turned back towards the window, causing Austin's hand to fall away. "I want you to know, I tried. Really I did. But I just need to know. It's the not knowing that's driving me insane."

My words met with silence, so I pushed forward. "When you thought I was dead … did you … I mean … were you with anyone else … sexually?" The question was finally out, hanging there between us, and my gut roiled. "I'm sorry, I just need to know. I can't stand not knowing anymore."

When Austin still didn't respond, I risked a glance at him from under my eyelashes. He sat perfectly still, his jaw clenched, and guilt etched into every line on his face. My heart fisted painfully in my chest. Maybe I didn't actually want to know.

"Never mind," I mumbled. "Maybe I can't handle the truth."

"I love you, Sam. You're my Sammy girl—my good Sammy girl. And you're the only woman I ever have and ever will love. That's all you need to know." His voice cracked slightly. "What happened when I thought you were dead doesn't matter. I never stopped loving you."

My world became blurry behind a wall of water, the hot tears spilling down my cheeks a moment later. "I hate him. So much."

"Malcolm's dead. You don't have—"

"No! Not Malcolm—Nixon." I choked back a sob. "All of this is his fault. And to think him and I … me and him … we lived like husband and wife for all that time. I-I-I hate him."

Every time Nixon touched me, kissed me—fucked me,

I willingly betrayed Austin. It didn't matter that I didn't know. I let all of it happen. I'd left myself vulnerable to be preyed upon. All the blame couldn't sit squarely on Nixon's shoulders since he'd merely taken advantage of a situation I created for him.

Austin wrapped his arms around me tightly, and I sucked in a shuddering breath, inhaling his scent. "Don't think about it. Any of it. We're together now, and the rest of it doesn't matter anymore."

My body quivered and shook as I sobbed, my anxiety refusing to let go even as I concentrated on trying to steady my breathing. *In two, out three, in two, out three ...*

"Sam, please." I knew Austin wasn't just pleading with me to calm down, to stop crying, but rather to let it go—all of it.

And I wanted to, more than anything in that moment, but I just wasn't sure I could.

Unable to help myself, I whispered, "How many?"

Austin's body tensed around mine, his fingers digging into my shoulders almost painfully.

Gritting my teeth, I demanded with more force, "How many?"

"Don't ask me that. Please."

"Why? Because I won't like the answer?" And I knew I wouldn't. But I'd already gone beyond the point of no return. He had to sense that I wouldn't let any of it go until I got the answers I needed.

Tell me, damn it!

"Why are you doing this? Why do you need to know?"

"I just do."

"Why, Sam? I know you were with Nixon." Austin's hands slid into my hair, fists forming. "But I don't want to know about it. Hell, even talking about it now makes me want to break things. Why torture yourself needlessly?"

"Because you know I was with Nixon, you just don't know the details. I don't know who you were with … and I need to know. I can't explain why, but I just do."

"Fine," Austin growled.

I mentally braced myself for what was to come, my heart thrumming wildly.

"I was with … I-I just can't Sam." His grip on my hair tightened painfully, but it didn't begin to compare with the agony in my heart. "If I tell you, it will be acknowledging it happened and I don't want to. I can't."

Pulling away from Austin, I let the fury in my eyes blaze forth. "You know when you let loose the reins on my powers, I'll just go in and pull it out of your mind. If I do it that way, I'll see details … details that I don't want, details that might break me."

Austin shook his head slowly, anguish rolling through his eyes before he closed them. "I won't let you into that part of my mind. I won't let you see."

"As if you'll be able to stop me."

His eyes snapped open, and his lips curled up into a smirk. "I'll always be more powerful than you, Sammy. Better get used to it now."

"Bullshit."

His smirk morphed into a grin, showcasing his

dimples. "I don't know what the dynamic between you and Nixon was, but that should have been your first clue."

Austin cupped my face, his large palm cradling my cheek. My body bade me to accept his touch, and I did, although I continued to glare at him.

"I'll always be stronger than you, and I'll always be on top—unless I want you there."

The double entendre wasn't lost on me.

"You're an asshole," I hissed.

"Yeah, but I'm your asshole, and you love me."

I hated how I wanted to hit him and climb on top of him simultaneously. How did one man manage to infuriate me and turn me on in practically the same breath, and with such ease?

"Looks like we're here." Austin stood abruptly and strode down the aisle towards the front of the plane.

How the hell did I miss our landing? Oh yeah, I was completely focused on Austin, as usual. "Don't go thinking this conversation is over!" I called after him, but he ducked out of the plane without so much as a backwards glance in my direction.

Chapter 5

Death's essence hovered in the air, its dark energy clinging to the remnants of life. A once-tall building lay in rubbles, scorch marks spreading out like fingerprints, marking the scene with death's dishonorable intentions. Dozens of bodies were somewhere inside, but instead of being horrified, I shivered with anticipation.

What kind of emotions lingered in the wake of all those lives? Their worries, fears, regrets … I would be able to sense all of it, connecting me to the dearly departed in an almost intimate way, and yet I would exist beyond them. That in itself made me feel almost invincible—beyond the reach of normal physical laws. I would experience death dozens of times over, all at once, and walk away without a scratch on me. It would be an unbelievable high.

"I can't let you do this." Austin's deep voice interrupted my reverie.

"It's not your call."

"Sam, look at me." Austin wrenched me around to face him, forcing me to meet his gaze.

I notched my chin up with defiance. "I'm the only one who can glean any useful information from all those people. It's not like I'm killing them. They're already dead, and it needs to be done."

"For now. You're not killing anyone—for now. I won't let you become like Malcolm." Austin's voice vibrated with anger, tension rolling off of him in palpable waves. "No one's life, or death, is worth more to me than yours."

"What happened to you telling me that you would do anything not to lose me? Including killing someone every single day if that's what I needed to survive. What happened to loving me unconditionally? Because," my voice cracked, "what if it's already too late?"

Austin cupped the back of my neck, his fingers splaying out in a possessive and yet comforting manner. He dropped his forehead to lean against mine, his dark gaze boring into me with determination. "I meant what I said. But it's not too late, Sam. Not yet."

I flicked my gaze away from his, slumping forward. "You're wrong. I feel the darkness inside of me growing. It wants out—No." I shook my head slightly. "It needs out. It's more than an addiction, it's a compulsion."

I returned my gaze to him, his features wavering from the tears building in my eyes. I blinked them back ferociously, refusing to let them fall. "I only hold off because I still know on some level that it's wrong, and I don't think I could actually kill someone for that high. But when it's there, like this," I waved my hand feebly behind me at the scorched land and rubble, "I can practically taste their deaths already, and my body is hungering for it."

"I'll help you then," Austin whispered. His words were a lifeline I wanted to grab onto, but I was afraid if I took what he was offering I'd pull him down with me instead of him pulling me up.

"I won't let you become tainted like me."

"You're not tainted," Austin growled. "And together we can handle anything." He stepped away from me, giving me a cocky grin. "Or we'll both enjoy our ride to hell together."

"Austin," I chastised, "you shouldn't joke about—"

He was suddenly in front of me, his lips slanting over mine possessively. When he let me go, the only thing I had on my mind was him, which I'm sure was his intention.

He grinned. "See, you and me—that's all that matters. The rest is insignificant."

"Maybe," I mumbled.

"So it's settled. I'm helping."

"That remains to be seen." I pushed past him, my stomach in knots.

Making my way over to the rubble, I surveyed the scene and who was working it. The few cops and rescue workers still there were under the impression that Austin and I were some kind of specialists. What kind? I wasn't exactly sure, but it didn't matter as long as they continued to ignore us. Just to be on the safe side, I knelt down and pretended to look at something on the ground.

Austin pressed in behind me, resting his hand on my shoulder. "You ready?"

"As I'll ever be." Trembling, I sucked in a few ragged breaths, anticipation surging through me, causing my heart rate to spike. All those deaths, and the freedom feeling them would bring me, would be nothing short of sublime.

The emotional barrier Austin had resurrected around me, keeping my empath gifts at bay, came crashing down.

Bits and pieces of emotions and thoughts pummeled my senses. *Surprise: "What the hell was that?" Shock: "It can't be—no!" Denial: "This can't be happening. Not here. Not now. I refuse to die."* But every thought, every emotion was followed by the shadow of imminent death. Some died slowly, at least in comparison to the nearly instantaneous deaths, and others barely had time to process what was happening. The most intoxicating deaths were the ones that burned alive. Sick, I know. But to feel that level of agony in a removed sort of way, to experience the terror, and then finally the euphoria that one's final breath would bring because it was a relief—an escape from the pain … bliss, complete bliss for them and me.

And now Austin was feeling it all right along with me.

Without opening my eyes or letting go of the death surrounding us, I turned and wiggled my way into Austin's arms. I pressed my nose into his shirt, inhaling his spicy scent. Pushing onto my tiptoes, I slid my face into the curve of his neck. His heart beat in unison with mine, the rhythm fast and steady. He shuddered against me, the joy of his journey through death disorienting for him, but nonetheless enjoyable. We were linked, the three of us—him, me, and death. As I siphoned from death's offerings, Austin reveled in the emotions through me, his world opening to what I'd already been forced to discover ... that another's end is the perfect high for the living.

The death echoes came to an end, much like racers in a marathon staggering across the finish line, and as soon as the last one made it, Austin and I were left alone with the afterglow.

"Holy shit," he rumbled, his hands clenched in my shirt.

"Exactly," I murmured, not caring in the least where we were. All I wanted in that moment was to ride out my high with Austin inside of me. And because he was still in my mind, I knew he wanted the same.

"Fuck! It ... that was ..." Austin couldn't find words to express what he was feeling in that moment, but he didn't need to. Words from him were not what I wanted.

After ripping his shirt over his head, I roughly grabbed for the buttons on his jeans. "Now, Austin! I need you now."

His eyes snapped open, the blue in them blazing with the kind of intensity that only made me want to get him naked faster.

"They won't see us." He answered the question before I could even think it.

He couldn't make us invisible, per se, but Austin could manipulate people's emotions so they'd look past us, not see us because they wouldn't care to observe us. It was quite a nifty little trick, and it was all the permission I needed.

Our hands tore at each other's clothes, and before I had time to perceive what I was doing, I had Austin on his back on the ground, and I was riding us both to our releases right there in front of everyone—even though they technically didn't know what we were doing.

I was alive … so, so alive. Those deaths brought with them a euphoria that wasn't like anything I'd ever experienced before, and to add kindling to the fire, the love of my life was currently buried deep inside of me, sharing everything—connecting us in a way we'd never felt before. *Heaven.*

"Sam, Sam, Sam ... my Sammy girl," Austin's voice whispered in my mind. *"Never stop. Need you."*

His thoughts were fragmented, desperate. Regardless, I knew what he meant, and I felt the same way. *"Never. I'll never stop loving you, touching you. Because you're mine. And I'm yours."*

Death—all those deaths, and us linked as we felt them only served to heighten the frantic need to lose ourselves in each other. He thought I was dead only a short time ago, and I thought he was a figment of my imagination. But now, in this moment, none of that mattered. Having walked away from those deaths made us feel our lives more acutely—making us want to grab onto each other and never let go. Nothing else mattered but us, together in this moment. He was my world, and I was his—and I needed to feel him … feel all of him, mind, body, and soul.

I screamed my release in perfect unison with Austin's, but there was no reprieve from my excessive need for him. The flames of my desire crackled and burned, reaching higher. I needed more … more … more.

My hands roamed his sweat-glistening body, and my lips continued to sip at the sweet nectar that was his mouth. "Austin," I moaned. "Please."

"Yeah. Yeah, I'm with you, Sam. I'm with you," he murmured against my lips. He continued to pivot his hips until he stiffened inside of me with fresh excitement.

"Yes … yes … yes …" I repeated on an unending loop, losing myself in Austin completely, because he would always be exactly what I needed.

INHALING SLOWLY, I let Austin's scent envelop me. His heart thrummed steadily under my ear, his chest rising and falling evenly. I attempted to snuggle closer to him, but my entire body ached with the kind of soreness that only came from extreme physical exertion. Groaning, my eyes fluttered open.

A hotel. We were in a hotel, and a pretty nice one if my

eyes weren't deceiving me. But how did we get here? The last thing I remembered was …

Austin and I locked together, writhing in ecstasy, him taking me in every possible way imaginable—over and over again—lost in the high brought on from us feeling the deaths from the bomb scene. I shuddered involuntarily, disgusted by our reactions to the deaths. And yet … yet I didn't regret the intense pleasure we'd shared afterwards.

I rubbed my temples. *That's right.* We'd stumbled back to this hotel after leaving the crime scene, drunk on the death reverb euphoria, and wanting nothing more than to slake our needs with each other.

"Sammy," Austin's sex-roughened voice broke the silence, his hand flexing against my naked back. "What happened?" He slid out from under me and propped himself up on his elbow.

Biting my lip, I met his gaze briefly before my attention darted over him, taking in how his hair was disheveled in the most appealing way, and his jaw sported just the right amount of scruff. His slightly rumpled appearance had me assessing my current state, and groaning internally in annoyance when I realized how sore I was.

After clearing my throat, I said, "What do you remember?" *Focus. Do not think about running your tongue over his delectable abs. And definitely don't think about climbing on top of him to— Nope. Don't. Don't think about any of that.*

His eyes glazed over as he went intrinsic to search his memories. "Not much, just a lot of us having sex." A lazy grin spread across his face. "Which was—"

"Yeah," I breathed.

Reaching up to thread my hands in his silky locks, I tugged his face down to meet mine. *Hmmm ... maybe I'm not that sore. I mean, I don't need to walk today.* Austin's lips claimed my mouth briefly before he moved his way down my body. I moaned when he captured my nipple between his teeth, biting gently.

A sharp knock at the door reverberated through the room, but only when it morphed into a steady pounding did Austin stop his ministrations.

"What the fuck?" Austin growled.

He jumped to his feet, scanning the room for our clothes. Once he located a pair of boxers, he pulled them on and grabbed a robe from the bathroom for me before heading to the door.

"Who is it?" he ground out, his eyes flashing with annoyance.

"Open up, man. It's me, Taryn."

Austin confirmed through the peephole before unlocking the door. I barely managed to finish belting my robe when the door exploded inward, banging against the wall. Taryn and Nixon strode in, Nixon being the reason Austin hadn't been able to sense who was on the other side of the door.

"No. He's not welcome here," Austin grated, taking a menacing step towards Nixon.

Taryn intercepted him by coming to stand in between the two men. Nixon pushed the door shut, turning his gaze towards me before flicking it away.

"I'm going to cut right to the chase," Taryn spoke steadily. "You've been missing for two days, and during that time things have gone completely off the rails."

I gaped at Taryn. *Two days? We've been missing for two days?* I glanced at Austin, noting that he was wearing a similar shocked expression.

Taryn chuckled darkly. "Yeah, I thought you two would react that way."

"While the two of you have been off having the time of your lives, apparently," Nixon spat, "things have been falling apart. Natalie's missing ... presumed dead."

"What?" Austin and I said in unison.

My mind was still reeling from the revelation that I'd been having sex for two days straight basically. *Fuck. No wonder I'm sore. And what about food? We couldn't have survived for two days with what we ate off each other. That would be impossible, but—*

"And I'm in charge now," Nixon added.

My head whipped up to meet his gaze as a smug smile spread across his face.

"You and Austin have ten minutes to gather your things and to come with us—no questions asked—or you're both off the team. And with what the two of you have been up to, I can guarantee you won't like the results of that decision."

My blood heated as fury surged through my system. I bared my teeth in a snarl. "Are you threatening us?"

"Yes, I am."

A red haze slipped over my vision, and with a bellow of rage, I rushed Nixon like a feral cat, my fingers extended like claws. "How dare you!"

But Austin snagged me around the waist, yanking me against his chest before I could make contact with Nixon. Even as I thrashed in his arms, he said, "We'll be ready."

I whipped my head around to glare at him, and he spoke directly into my mind. "*Trust me.*"

Obviously, Austin was picking up on something I wasn't. Grinding my teeth, I nodded once in acknowledgment. But even though I was going to go along with Austin because I would always trust him, I still didn't like it. Not one little bit.

Chapter 6

"You're actually serious? You want to get married in Vegas? Like by some Elvis impersonator or something?"

"Yep," Austin said, a grin pulling his mouth impossibly wide. "If you want something more traditional later, that's fine, but I want to make you my wife as soon as possible." He tossed me over his shoulder and carried me the short distance from the bed to the closet. "Now start packing."

"You might need to put me down first, genius." I giggled when Austin smacked my ass.

"I kind of like you where you are," he murmured. He set me on my feet despite his words.

I reached up, tracing my fingers along his jaw before threading my fingers in his messy hair. "I can't believe you want to marry me."

Austin's azure gaze met my green one with intensity. "That's exactly why I want to do it as soon as possible, so you won't doubt us anymore. I love you, my Sammy girl, and I want you, along with the rest of the world, to know it."

It was hard to believe sometimes that Austin had been such a player, especially when he said things like that to me. "I love you, too," I whispered, pulling his head down to capture his lips with mine.

"Sam, wake up. We're about to land."

"Huh?" I blinked and then rubbed my blurry eyes. Groaning, I gingerly twisted my neck to the side. I'd fallen asleep at an odd angle with my head tucked against the window.

"What were you dreaming about?" Austin smiled, leaning in closer to me, his warm breath fanning my cheek. "It was difficult to resist taking a little peek, especially when I was picking up on your happy emotions." His nostrils flared. "I could use some of those right about now."

I dragged my lower lip between my teeth before smiling softly. "I was dreaming about our wedding—or us getting ready to go to Vegas anyways, not the actual ceremony. Sometimes I still dream memories. Thankfully, it's mostly happy ones now."

And the rest of the time they're about my time with Malcolm, I silently tacked on as my smile drooped into a frown. "But we don't have time to reminisce about such things. We need to figure out what happened with us and what else is going on." Hopefully, Austin would think my mood turning sour was from those topics and not thoughts of Malcolm.

Austin's jaw ticked with tension as he spoke directly into my mind. "*We need to not rock the boat for now, just go along with whatever is happening until we can figure out the best course of action. We're in a very precarious position at the moment. I just haven't figured out how bad off we are yet.*"

Nodding, I intertwined my fingers with his as the plane touched down.

The flight attendant opened the small door, signaling we were all clear to go. Taryn and Nixon stood immediately, and Austin and I trailed behind them at a slower pace. The two of us were both hesitant to accept Nixon's leadership for obvious reasons, but knew we had to get all the facts before we ended up screwing ourselves over worse than we already had.

As we exited the plane, I spotted two darkened sedans waiting on the tarmac. Nixon said something tersely to Taryn, and Taryn then turned towards Austin and me. "Sam's riding with me, and you're going with Nixon."

"No," I snapped, gripping Austin's hand tighter. "Absolutely not."

Nixon's void power settled around us like a blanket, ratcheting up my anxiety. The fact that he was trying to separate us—that detail pointed at nothing good, that was for sure.

Austin squeezed my hand before letting it drop. "It'll be fine, Sam. At least I'm the one riding with Nixon. Maybe he just doesn't want to deal with the emotions the two of us being together brings up in him … maybe he's attempting to be professional."

I glanced over at Nixon as he ducked into the back of the closest sedan. "No, it's something else."

"I can handle him," Austin replied with a slight smirk. "Just go with Taryn and I'll see you in a few."

Austin's lips touched mine briefly before he turned and stalked over to the same sedan Nixon had just disappeared into. My stomach gurgled, acid churning as dread pushed its way through my system. I couldn't stand the thought of being separated from Austin, even for a short time. Not with the current situation.

Frozen in place, I couldn't seem to peel my eyes away even as the door shut with a firm click. *Please, please just get out of there and then we can ... what? What can we do? Run? Austin's right. We need to get more information before we inadvertently do something stupid.*

"Taryn," I squeaked, but wasn't quite sure what I wanted to say.

"It'll all be fine, Sam," Taryn said gruffly before turning to enter the sedan we'd be riding in.

I slid into the cool, dark interior and inhaled the leather smell. Wrapping my arms around myself, I eyed Taryn's large body folded up in the opposite corner. Glancing to the front of the car, I briefly wondered who our driver was, but dismissed him quickly. I needed to get some answers from Taryn. With Nixon in the other sedan, I, at least, was able to use my empath abilities to aid me in my endeavor.

"Taryn, talk to me, please," I whispered.

His muscles coiled with tension, but he remained

silent, his gaze carefully averted from mine. I knew he heard me though, and I watched him intently as he pushed a chunk of black hair that had escaped his ponytail behind his ear.

He sighed heavily, his shoulders sagging slightly. "Things have gone to shit. There's not much else to say."

Waves of anxiety rolled off of Taryn, and I ground my teeth together as I tried to keep them from affecting me. "What happened to Natalie? Why is Nixon suddenly in charge? How'd you find us? You have to give me something, goddamn it!"

Taryn tilted his head, his amber eyes meeting mine with confusion. "After you and Austin went missing, we got reports of the blast, and then Natalie went missing soon after that. Those things are all connected, that much is for sure. As for Nixon being in charge, there's protocol and—"

"Wait, wait, wait!" I cut my hand through the air and narrowed my eyes at Taryn. "What do you mean you got reports about the blast *after* Austin and I went missing? Natalie sent us to check out the scene to find out ..." Taryn's lips parted as he regarded me with surprise. "Natalie sent us," I finished up numbly. Something wasn't right beyond what I had initially thought. Anxiety tightened its grip on my chest.

Taryn shook his head slowly, his gaze never wavering from mine. "No. Why would she do that with you being in your condition? She made it quite clear to everyone that you needed some time away from death scenes."

Icy claws of dread sliced down my spine. "Tell me what's really going on, Taryn."

"Don't worry, Sam. You're safe. Either way, Nixon isn't holding you responsible. He just—"

"Austin … he thinks Austin had something to do with the blast? Y-You can't be serious." Was Nixon that much of a vindictive asshole that he'd blame Austin for something he didn't do to rip him out of my life again? I never would have believed it in the past but …

My heart exploded in my chest, and I struggled to breathe. Lurching forward, I slapped my hand against the window. "Oh my— Fuck! He can't … he wouldn't— What'll happen if Austin gets pinned for this crime?"

"If he just took you there to feed your … cravings, then not a whole lot, but if he caused the blast—"

Shoving off my seat, I crowded into Taryn's space, screeching, "He would never do either of those things! You know he wouldn't!"

Taryn recoiled, sinking as far as he could into his seat. Finally registering his reaction, I slouched back into mine, sucking in ragged breaths.

Just as I managed to get myself under control, Taryn said, "There's evidence."

"Bullshit! Fucking bullshit! There's no fucking evidence! Can't you see? It's Nixon … he's doing this. I don't know how, but he is!" I smashed my fists into the soft leather on either side of me several times, wishing it was Nixon's face.

If he does anything to Austin … if he hurts him in any way

– *No.* I shook my head. *Even he wouldn't go that far, would he?* Maybe he wouldn't hurt him physically, but with the resources now at his fingertips the possibilities of what he could do were terrifying.

"Tell me this ..." My voice was surprisingly calm. I somehow even managed to uncurl my fists. "Is Nixon trying to blame Austin for Natalie's disappearance, too?"

Taryn was turned completely away from me as if he was trying to pretend I didn't exist in that moment.

My calm veneer shattered. "Tell me! Just tell me what the fuck will happen!"

Taryn mumbled something as he forced his large body closer to the window, but I didn't need to hear his words —I felt his emotions. And I garnered the stark truth from them. If Austin was found guilty of his alleged crimes, he would be put to death. That was the real reason we'd been separated, so we wouldn't be able to run. Nixon was trying to hijack my life again. But this time I was ready for him, and I would make him pay.

Yes, I'll make Nixon pay. For this and everything else he's done.

White-hot rage erupted within me, exploding out in all directions. My fury rippled the air like heat waves as it flew towards its targets. Taryn let out a yelp of pain just as the sedan swerved, lurching to a sudden stop.

After fumbling with the door handle, I spilled out onto the side of the road in a heap, my heart thundering in my ears. Random cars whizzed past us on the highway, but there was no other sedan in sight.

No, no, no, no, no. I shoved my mind in Austin's direction, needing to feel him—assure myself that he was okay, at least until I could get to him. And even though I knew that it would be nearly impossible to connect with him because of Nixon using his void ability, the frustration of failing nearly suffocated me.

That's when one word broke through my consciousness loud and clear. "*Run.*"

Without a second thought, I turned and fled down the side of the road in the direction of oncoming traffic as fast as my legs would carry me.

Forcing oxygen into my burning lungs, I willed my exhausted body to continue running—pushing myself to the limit until my fatigued muscles finally gave out on me and I collapsed on the side of the road. I clawed at the ground, my vision wavering and my mind slipping into unconsciousness.

Austin. Please.

TREMBLING UNCONTROLLABLY, my eyelids fluttered open, and I noted that the day had slid into night, the air chilly now that the sun had set. In my mad dash to safety, I'd somehow made my way off the road and into a small patch of woods nearby. I wasn't sure how long I'd been lying there or how I hadn't been found yet, but I wasn't going to question my good fortune in that respect.

Stumbling to my feet, I swayed slightly as I surveyed

my surroundings. A sudden burst of wind gusted over my exposed skin, causing fresh goose bumps to erupt. I rubbed my arms to warm up as I began to shake again.

Car headlights flickered between the trees as they sped down the highway, causing my vision to waver. Dizziness and disorientation kept me from being able to completely focus. I had no idea what I was doing, but I knew I had to come up with some kind of plan and fast. Austin's life was in danger, and it was up to me to save him. For that, I knew I needed answers, but first I needed to get myself somewhere off grid.

Ambling farther into the woods, I abruptly froze in place. *Wait. This is exactly what Nixon will expect. He knows me. After all, he did play my husband for years. I need to do the unexpected if I want to have any hope at all.* I pivoted on my heels and dashed back to the side of the road, waving my arms frantically.

A few minutes passed before a black pickup truck screeched to a halt a few feet from me. The window rolled down, revealing the backlit silhouette of an elderly man.

"Need help, darlin'?" a thick southern drawl slid out into the night air.

"Yes." I nodded my head enthusiastically. "I need a ride, I had some trouble … car trouble."

"Hop in, I'll give you a ride then. It's not safe to be on the side of the road at night by yourself. Especially as a woman."

For most people, it wouldn't be much safer accepting a ride from a stranger either, but most people couldn't attack a potential threat with their mind if they needed to.

After yanking the truck's door open, I hopped into the cab. Once inside, I got a better look at my roadside savior. He was indeed elderly like I'd thought, with an unruly mop of white hair that framed a friendly face and smile. After a quick survey of his emotions, I determined him to be a genuinely nice person who just wanted to help a stranger in need. I'd gotten lucky with my rare find.

"Thanks," I mumbled, averting my gaze and folding my hands demurely in my lap.

"Where can I drop you?" he asked as he maneuvered back into traffic.

Now that's a very good question. I needed supplies and a plan. But first I needed a safe place to work from, a home base of sorts, while I figured everything out. But where could I go that Nixon wouldn't know to—

"It's not that difficult of a question," the man stated. "You in some kind of real trouble, darlin'?"

Again, I stayed silent, not knowing how to respond. My mind seemed sluggish and I began to wonder if maybe I was suffering from some kind of shock.

My stomach cramped, and I lurched forward, sweat beads forming on my forehead. *Something is wrong. Something is very wrong.* First, I'd been freezing, and now I was burning up. And it was like my mind was stuck in molasses.

Am I drugged? Did Nixon have me drugged before I escaped, hoping to subdue me? But when? How? My vision blurred, and that's when acceptance finally hit. I, somehow, was in fact drugged, and when I collapsed on the side of the road, it wasn't from exhaustion. No, it was from whatever drug currently coursing through my system.

"Drugged ... I've been drugged. I ..."

Everything went dark.

Chapter 7

Fingertips skimmed along my cheekbone and drew a feather-light trail down my jawline. Warm breath tickled my ear. "Sam, I love you." Austin's deep voice echoed through my mind.

It's not real. He's not actually here with me. The agony of his absence left me hollow and numb, my heart a brick in my chest.

"Should we call an ambulance or take her to the hospital?" An elderly woman's voice made its way into my consciousness as I began to wake up.

"She was runnin', darlin'. And she's been drugged. Her vitals are all fine. I think it's best if we don't involve the authorities, for her sake, at least until we get her side of the story." I recognized the voice of the man from the truck.

Relief swept through me as my eyes fluttered open. By some stroke of good luck, I'd gotten a reprieve by stumbling into the right truck, almost quite literally. I wondered if Nixon was frantically searching for me right now, the thought tugging the corners of my mouth into a small smile.

"I'm fine. Please don't call anyone," I croaked. "Someone that I love … more than anything—" I swallowed around the boulder in my throat. "His life depends on me staying undetected for the moment."

Pushing myself up onto my elbows, I realized I was lying on a couch. The man from the truck was standing close by, next to a petite elderly woman with silver hair pulled into a loose bun. They both looked very rustic—very mom and pop Kent. Their emotions felt good to me, warm and soothing … pure somehow.

I'll be safe with them for now.

"You see, she's fine." The man smiled at the woman. Then he addressed me, "Tell us what's going on, if you can."

I nodded, my tongue thick and heavy in my mouth from whatever drug I'd been given. "I'll explain as much as I can. I owe you both that much for helping me. But first, can I have some water, please? My throat—" I coughed lightly, unable to hold it back any longer.

"Of course," the man replied as the woman scurried off without a word, to return swiftly with a tall glass of cold water for me. She smiled gently as she handed it to me. I idly noted that they both seemed pretty spry for how old they appeared.

My eyes slid shut briefly as I gulped down the water. "Thank you."

"You're welcome, darlin'," the man said. "Now, whenever you're ready."

They both peered at me expectantly, their emotions impatient.

"Well, um … yes. The whole situation, what I'm involved in … it's all very complicated, and the less you know the better, but … okay …"

What could I tell them? Partial truths would work best since they would come off as the most sincere, especially since even the watered-down version of my story was going to be hard to swallow.

"My ex-boyfriend drugged me."

The man frowned, and the woman gasped.

"He's trying to pin a crime on my husband to get him out of the way. He drugged me … well, I think so I can't get the evidence that I need to prove my husband's innocence. It's—" I shifted uncomfortably. "It's all very complicated, like I said because all of us work for the government. I can't give you any more details about that part." I swallowed and looked away. It wasn't a lie exactly and it helped to illustrate the high stakes. "It's probably best if I leave as soon as possible, they're already trying to track me down, I have no doubt."

Silence hung awkwardly for a few heartbeats before the man cleared his throat. "I'm Paul, and this is my wife, Wendy. Where can I take you?"

Surprise shot through me. "You don't think I'm crazy?"

Rifling through his emotions, I found that no, indeed he did not.

Wendy chuckled. "No, my husband and I are a bit of conspiracy theorists. Besides, what do we have to lose besides a bit of time, and maybe some gas money?"

Sudden optimism buoyed me. Clearly, luck was on my side, and finding Paul and Wendy under the circumstances had to be a good sign of things to come. At least that's what I was going to believe.

I'd been through worse—so much worse in my life. There was no way on hell or earth that I'd lose Austin again, especially after just getting him back. And if anyone tried to stand in my way, they would suffer my wrath.

GAZING INTO THE MIRROR, I didn't recognize the person staring back at me. It went beyond the physical, and my newly darkened hair. The issue was within my eyes—and the haunted look in them. When I'd been forced to spend time with Malcolm, I often peered into my eyes and swore that I saw the darkness he'd awakened in them … the taint on my soul reflected back at me. After being reunited with Austin, I allowed myself to ignore it—to pretend it no longer existed. Now, I had to face the truth, which was not only was I tainted, but I had somehow permitted it to touch Austin, and if I didn't stop it, I would ruin him in the same way I was.

I conjured a recent memory of the two of us after siphoning the death emotions from the blast sight …

Every nerve ending in my skin was exposed ... raw, and Austin's callused fingers seemed to hold electricity in them, shocking my senses with each caress of my body. He handled me roughly, nearly crossing the pain-pleasure threshold, but not quite. As he plunged into me over and over, giving me no quarter, I cried out for more, more, more ... I would always want more, and I would never have enough of him. Ever. Austin was a part of me, and now we shared everything ... love and death intermingled, light and dark embracing us in perfect harmony. I could no longer tell where I ended and he began, we were linked irrevocably. If there was ever a question before, there was none now. There was no turning back for us. His lips branded me, and his tongue soothed my aching flesh ...

Wrenching myself from the carnal memory, I forced myself to concentrate on the here and now. And yet, my mind again turned back to what we'd shared. I yearned for that level of closeness with him—the all-consuming connection. For so long, I'd been deprived of just that, and even when we'd been reunited physically, I had to suffer the distance of our mental connection when Austin had kept me shut off from my empath abilities. The time we spent together after the blast scene had been the most amazing of my life, and yet the most terrifying because of its implications.

And now he's gone. Completely. Not here physically or mentally. Just gone.

I narrowed my eyes at my reflection. “Stop feeling sorry for yourself because you’re going to get him back.”

In this, the girl in the mirror and me were in agreement. Austin wouldn’t die, we would save him at any cost. And thanks to Paul and Wendy, the slightly paranoid elderly couple, I had a place to stay, some money, and a new look. It wasn’t much but it was something, and better than the situation Nixon expected me to be in.

Turning from the mirror, I heaved a huge sigh and pulled on the cheap cotton pajama bottoms and tank top Wendy purchased for me to sleep in. I was laying low in a small apartment above their garage for the night. I wished I didn’t have to, but I needed at least one decent night’s rest before I set out on my quest for answers slash rescue mission.

Barely aware of my surroundings because of my physical and emotional fatigue, I collapsed onto the small day bed that smelled slightly of mildew. I found myself almost instantly in dreamland.

Chapter 8

Her vision was fixed and blurred, her chest heaving, her breathing labored. Ice seemed to encase her limbs. All the fight had drained from her body. She was dying and there was nothing left for her aside from acceptance. I smiled as I inhaled on her last exhale, a beautiful dance of life and death—she died and I lived—me feeling all that much more alive from her exit of this mortal coil. It was as if only so much light could shine in this world, and by her light being extinguished, mine got to shine brighter. Perfection. That moment in time was complete and utter perfection. But then he *laughed, his merriment beating against my eardrums and causing me to cry out in frustration.*

"Sam, you're the perfect student. Every time I feel you enjoying the deaths as much as I do, I'm overcome with anticipation, wondering how much Austin will be horrified." Malcolm's laugh surrounded me, never-ending in its torment.

Pissed, that's what I was. Pissed off at the entire

fucking world. Since suffering from yet another series of dreams about my time with Malcolm, I was left in a state of rage. It simmered within me, threatening to boil over at the slightest provocation.

Instead of waking up alone in a strange bed, I should have been in Austin's loving embrace. We'd lost so much time together because of Malcolm, and his essence still haunted me, threatening to separate us again thanks to the dark cravings he'd helped to nurture in me. Hell, if I could bring Malcolm back to life and kill him over and over again … well, that'd be a death I'd have no guilt over enjoying.

Murderous thoughts continued to plague me regarding Malcolm, a man who was already dead. The whole thing was pointless, and yet I couldn't seem to get my fury under control.

I ground my teeth together while I gathered the few items I could currently claim as my own … some clothes and toiletries. I had no identification, no real money, only what Paul and Wendy could spare. Even after a fitful night's sleep, I didn't have a concrete plan of what my next step should be. Knowing that I had to track down information about Natalie and or find her wasn't really more than a plan to have a plan. Where was I headed and how would I get there exactly?

As I stepped out of the front door of the small apartment, I nearly tripped over a rolled-up newspaper. I picked it up, idly wondering why it was there. Shouldn't it have been delivered to the main house? But what did I know, maybe Paul and Wendy had previously rented out the small space to someone and they hadn't discontinued the service yet.

Part of a headline caught my attention through the plastic '... *al Killer?*' I pulled the newspaper from its protective shell and read about the suspected serial killer in Ohio.

Here's the thing about people like me whose lives exist in a space beyond the ordinary: We usually don't believe in coincidences. When you ask a specific question, the universe usually provides you with an answer in some way, shape, or form. The newspaper had found its way into my hands for a reason, and now I knew where I was headed—Dayton, Ohio.

The problem was, I still wasn't sure how I was going to get there. Nixon, and whoever else he'd have out searching for me, were very good at tracking people down. Not to mention the bevy of nifty tech toys they had at their disposal. A new darker hair color and a hat wasn't going to help me fly under the radar. Plus, I couldn't get on a plane without a form of I.D., and even if I had some, I'd be spotted if I attempted to board a commercial flight. It was actually a small miracle that I hadn't been discovered yet.

"Sam," a familiar voice broke into my inner musings, freezing me in place about halfway up the gravel driveway.

Lifting my head, I met deep brown eyes filled with anger.

Fuckity, fuck, fuck, fuck. I'd spoken—or thought rather—too soon. Apparently, I was wrong, there was no miracle because I'd been discovered. "Nixon," I grated, tensing, ready to either run or fight.

He stood a few feet away with his arms hanging loosely at his sides. I recognized his stance; he was ready to either counter my attack or chase me down. We eyed each other warily.

"Nice dye job," Nixon said snidely, obviously referring to my freshly darkened hair. "You really thought we couldn't track you down?"

I quirked an eyebrow. "I had my doubts. Where's Austin?"

"He's safe … for now."

My nostrils flared as I fought back the urge to tackle him to the ground and pummel his face into bloody oblivion. "You can't actually believe that he had anything to do with that bomb, with those deaths?"

His jaw muscles jumped. "I never would have thought Malcolm capable of some of the things he did either—before he did them."

Was he actually trying to compare Austin to Malcolm? The idea was beyond insulting and completely ludicrous. "If anyone's capable of those types of things, it would be me. I'm the one who should be the prime suspect if it's between the two of—"

"No," Nixon snapped, cutting me off. "You would never do that."

Unbidden, my mind flashed to Austin and me reveling

in the beautiful death emotions from the blast sight. Sadness washed over me. "I wish that were true. Or maybe I couldn't do it now, but ..." I shook my head slowly, not wanting to admit my potential failings out loud, or even to myself really.

"I'm not going to let that happen, Sam."

I snorted. "Please, Nixon. We both know you're in denial. And you want to blame Austin for everything for obvious reasons, but you can't. It's all me. He was just trying to help. It's never been him, and it's always been me."

"I'm going to save you," Nixon whispered.

But his words only served to enflame me more. "I only have room for one man in my life with a hero complex and it's not you. I choose him. I don't love you, Nixon. I love Austin."

Holding his gaze, I took a step towards him. "Even if Austin was out of the picture," I waved a hand to motion between the two of us, "you and me are never going to happen. I'll never love you the way you want."

A cloud of dark emotions rolled across the surface of his eyes, dimming them. "You can't tell me that you didn't feel anything for me when we were together. I was there, I know you did."

"It wasn't you!" I sucked in a few ragged breaths before continuing. "Everything you made my body feel was based on my feelings for Austin. You replaced him in my memories with you. What I thought ... what I felt —" I clenched and unclenched my fists. "You hijacked my life. Everything. Every. Single. Thing—we had was a lie."

"I don't believe that. You loved me." He thumped his closed fist against his chest. "Me. You loved me. And I'm going to get you back."

Icy fingers of dread clamped around my heart. How far would he be willing to go to try and get me back? Would he kill Austin? Try to hijack my memories and therefore my life again? I might try to tell myself that it couldn't happen a second time, but if anyone had asked me years ago if it could happen at all, I would have said no.

"If you hurt him in any way, and I'm fucking serious, if it's your fault he even gets a papercut … I'll make you pay in unimaginable ways." I took another step closer to him. "And before you even consider the option of having my memories messed with again, look how well that worked out for you before. I didn't forget him, not really. And I'll know … my heart will know if he's gone. Just like it did before."

"Natalie's still missing. The evidence points to him, Sam. How sure are you of him, really? How much did he change in the years you were apart? Was he even faithful to you while you were gone?"

My gut roiled, acid pushing its way up my esophagus. That question was still left unanswered, and of course, Nixon would know how much the entire issue would be eating away at my insides. But in the end, it didn't matter. Austin thought I was dead. What he did with other women during that time—it would hurt, but it wouldn't stop me from loving him. So I pushed aside all thoughts of Austin naked, in bed with a bevy of beautiful women, refusing to address the subject at all with Nixon. I wouldn't make it that easy for him.

Obviously, threats weren't going to work, so I pivoted on my plan of attack. "If you ever loved me, then you'll give me a chance to prove his innocence. Please, Nixon. Prove to me the extent of your love."

A myriad of emotions rolled through his eyes as an internal war waged. But even though he had his void shield firmly in place, all the years we'd spent together living as husband and wife had made me adept at reading him. He was weighing what I said—how he could prove his love for me—against his other options. He wanted to give me what I wanted, but he also wanted me for himself. If he went along with me, therefore playing the long game as far as he was concerned, could he win me permanently in the end? Or did his original plan have a better chance of delivering him the results he wanted? He was considering all of it from every available angle.

His lips twitched into a frown, his decision made. "Fine," he grated. "I'll give you a chance, because knowing you, you probably already have a half-baked plan that you're going to find a way to do no matter the risk it'll put you in. And this is all about keeping you safe." Sighing, he ran a hand through his hair. "So what is it, Sam? Where were you headed just now?"

I didn't trust Nixon, not anymore anyways. But with

little choice, I had to make this small opportunity count. "Dayton, Ohio," I stated calmly.

Nixon's eyebrows shot up to almost his hairline. "Ohio? Why?"

"I'll explain on the way. Because I'm guessing I'm not going alone, am I?"

He snorted. "You got that right."

Chapter 9

Sitting shotgun next to Nixon, the man I thought was my husband for several years, then add in the fact that we were on our way to Ohio of all places … yep, it equaled a confusing, surreal situation, to say the least.

I studied Nixon's profile as daylight faded into dusk, and the soft glow of the streetlights illuminated his tense face. My emotions were a tangled knot of anxiety and confusion. Nixon had betrayed me on so many levels, which of course, infuriated me. But deep … deep, deep down I still held a bit of tenderness for him. He'd been kind and loving to me during our faux relationship. Supportive in ways that made him a better-than-average husband. And even though it came from a place of misplaced obsession, I knew he did love me. I could understand not wanting to let go … after all, it wasn't much different for me with Austin. The biggest contrast between the two situations was that Austin reciprocated my feelings.

Drumming my fingers idly on the door, I cleared my throat, the silence stifling. "You can't save me." When Nixon didn't respond, so much as flinch, I continued, "Are you hearing me? I can't be saved. Even if I could, it's not your responsibility to do it. Also, you need to stop blaming Austin for everything that's wrong with me. I—"

Nixon slammed his fist on the steering wheel. "If he would have just left you alone, then Malcolm never would have ..." He shook his head. "What I mean is— Fuck." He hit the steering wheel again. "If Austin could have just managed to stay away from you to begin with, then Malcolm never would have targeted you."

"But he couldn't stay away from me any more than I could from him. I pushed him. That's what you refuse to believe. The risk of being with him was ultimately my choice to make. Not his ... and certainly not yours." I gently laid my hand on his arm. "I love him, Nixon. And I'm sorry that I hurt you, but the heart wants what the heart wants."

Nixon's jaw muscles rippled as he ground his teeth together. "He's a liar and a cheat. He's no good for you."

I exhaled slowly through my nose. I didn't know why I was bothering. Nixon clearly didn't want to listen. But since I was forced to spend time with him, I didn't have anything to lose ... except maybe my sanity and temper. "I'm a liar and a cheat, too. I lied to you and cheated on you with Austin. I'm no good for you. Austin and I, we're just meant to be. You and I … are not."

"I'll do what's right when it comes to his life, but I'm not giving up on you, Sam. I can't."

Crossing my arms over my chest, I turned my gaze out the window, my patience wearing thin. What else could I possibly say to Nixon? I told him I loved Austin … over and over again. I was giving him zero hope of a future with me as far as I could tell. He needed to find someone who would love him the way he deserved, and it one hundred percent wasn't me.

"You going to tell me what this elusive evidence you claim to have on Austin is? Or how you ended up in charge of everything after Natalie's disappearance? And what about the fact that I haven't been able to feel Austin at all mentally since we got off that plane? Don't forget about—"

"Whoa. Slow down. And you already know there are things I can't tell you."

"You're in charge. You can tell me if you want to."

"No, Sam. I'm only in charge temporarily, there was protocol left behind for me to follow."

I glared at him. "How fucking convenient. So you're not going to give me anything?"

"Damn it, Sam, I am giving you something. I'm giving you a chance to prove whatever you're trying to prove by dragging me to goddamn fucking Ohio."

"Yes, because we've never tracked down a serial killer. Anyways … two birds, one stone."

I just hoped my instincts were right on this one. All I was going off of was a hunch from reading a newspaper article. In the end, if our little jaunt to Ohio didn't pan out, I was going to have to come up with a plan B to save Austin. As it was, I barely had a plan A.

Silence engulfed us again, both of us lost in our own thoughts. Soon, exhaustion pulled at me, and I leaned my head against the window. It wasn't long before I slipped into a restless sleep.

"Austin," I moaned, writhing against his hard body as he pressed me into the cold brick wall.

His hand slid up my thigh, disappearing under my dress. The warm metal band on his ring finger made me shiver with a different kind of pleasure.

"I can't believe we're married."

He hitched my leg around his hip as he ground himself into me. His feverish lips burned a path down my throat. "And Elvis married us."

I giggled at the memory. Winding my hands into his hair, I yanked his head back so I could look into his lust-filled eyes. "Maybe we should try and make it back to our hotel room. After all, I'm a married woman now."

"Great, married less than twenty minutes and you're already losing your adventurous side. Say it ain't so, my Sammy girl." Humor glinted in his eyes as a smirk tipped up one corner of his mouth.

I frowned. "Hey, not funny."

He pivoted his pelvis against me. "I call 'em like I see 'em." He dipped his head, nipping at my neck.

I groaned.

"I just thought it'd be nice to take advantage of our fancy hotel roo—" My words were effectively cut off as he pushed a finger inside of me.

"I need you now, Sam. I can't wait," Austin murmured against my skin.

Closing my eyes, I began to thrust my hips to the teasing rhythm of his fingers. "Mmmm ..." I mumbled incoherently.

"That's right. Love and obey me, wife," Austin said with a chuckle.

However, I couldn't have cared less what he was saying anymore, or about making it back to our hotel room either. I needed him inside of me as desperately as he wanted to be there. I cried out when he replaced his fingers with his hot and hard—

"Sam, wake the hell up," someone demanded, shaking me at the same time.

"What?" I snapped, squeezing my eyes shut tighter in an attempt to avoid reality.

Seriously, what the fuck? Annoyance nettled from being yanked from my delicious dream-memory of my wedding night with Austin. Unlike when my real memories had been stolen from me, I knew my dream had really happened. And I also was elated to have a reprieve from the nightmares of my time with Malcolm.

After another few moments of avoidance, I huffed out a sigh and blinked my bleary eyes into focus, my gaze alighting on Nixon. He was leaning over as far as he could go while still managing to drive, one hand on my shoulder.

Shirking out from his touch, I glared at him. "What the fuck, Nixon? Or am I not allowed to sleep anymore?"

"Not when you're saying his name in your sleep."

I gaped, completely stunned. "Austin?"

"Yeah," he ground out.

Recovering from my surprise, I narrowed my eyes at him. "So, I'm not permitted to dream about my husband in your presence?"

He withdrew his arm to his side of the car, then dragged his hand down his face. "Not that kind of dream."

"Oh, I'm sorry," I growled. "Soooo sorry that I was having a nice dream about my husband. I'll try to go back to having nightmares starring Malcolm again ... would that make you feel better?"

Nixon's face paled. "Do you—do you still have dreams about Malcolm?"

I ran my hands through my hair. "Yeah, it's what I dream about most of the time. They're memories from our time together."

"You mean you dream about ... the murders?" he asked hesitantly.

"Yes," I snapped. "So as you can see, I'm already broken, Nixon. You can stop trying to save me now."

"It's called post-traumatic stress disorder, Sam."

I raised my hand to silence him. "I liked feeling those deaths. More than liked it. And now, I crave it. I want more, so much more. Just without Malcolm." I smiled bitterly at him. "I wish I didn't, but there it is. I crave death emotions. It's too late to save me." I hated saying those words out loud, but if that's what it took to finally make him realize the truth then it would be worth it.

"It's never too late," Nixon murmured.

And with that, I finally gave up trying to convince him. Clearly, he knew that to be a lie from the evidence presented by dealing with Malcolm. Nixon's love for me was blinding him, and there was apparently nothing I could do about it. My only hope was to maybe use his feelings for me to help Austin.

We fell into silence—again—as we sped down the highway.

Chapter 10

The drive to Ohio was long and tension-filled, the hours steeped in silence. When we finally arrived in Dayton, a sense of optimism washed over me, which was highly unusual since I was a pessimist at heart. But as an empath, it was difficult not to be, having felt some of humanity's darkest emotions. I was able to see beyond people's public personas, always privy to what was hiding behind their carefully cultivated masks. True optimism, for me, or anyone else for that matter, was hard to come by.

Nixon promptly checked us into a mid-grade hotel room upon our arrival. After I insisted on two beds, he became inexplicably angry, and I wasn't in the headspace to peel back the layers on his issue with me needing space. If he thought anything physical, beyond me punching him in the face, was going to happen, he was more delusional than I'd originally thought. Not that I cared all that much since Nixon wasn't my priority and never would be again.

Rubbing my temples, I tried to force back the dull headache blooming along my skull. The truth was I didn't have much of a plan beyond getting myself to Ohio. Usually when on a case, the groundwork was laid out for me, some kind of plan already in place, but this time all I had was a vague hunch from a newspaper article.

Sighing heavily, Nixon flopped onto the small bed across from the one I was sitting cross-legged in. "Now what?"

I narrowed my eyes at him, not wanting to admit to my lack of foresight. "I'm working on it."

Nixon clicked his tongue and crossed his arms over his chest. "Isn't that typical of you? No plan but you rush right into things anyways?"

Biting the insides of my cheeks, I barely managed to contain the barrage of snide comments welling up within me. Even when I believed he was my husband, the subject of my rashness had been a point of contention, spawning many arguments between the two of us. I had a tendency to shoot first and ask questions later, so to speak. Of course, when I landed myself in hot water, Nixon was always the one coming to my rescue. Therefore, he wanted me to test the waters before I leapt in. Unfortunately, I was convinced I was born without patience when it came to such matters. And now, with Austin's life literally on the line, there would be no chance of me carefully planning anything out.

Taking in a few calming breaths, I reminded myself that Nixon wasn't my husband, and his opinion ultimately didn't matter. "Well, now that we're here it shouldn't be that hard to figure out the next step."

Nixon snorted.

My hands curled into fists, but I decided to pretend that he wasn't there, sitting on his bed, glaring at me. Sure, he was giving me a shot at finding evidence to clear Austin, but I also knew he wanted me to fail. He probably hoped that if he gave me a chance then I wouldn't blame him in the end, and he could be the one to comfort me once Austin was dead. I ground my teeth together. *Not going to happen. I'll kill you first, you deceitful bastard.*

Vibrating with anger, I closed my eyes as I forced my mind to let go, to wander past the images of bloodying Nixon's face. Soon my mind instinctively returned to the serial killer, the need to track them driving my focus.

What do I know about this serial killer? His or her killings have been escalating. They are most likely male though since the victims were all female, and statistically male serial killers are more common. The escalating part is the key factor. What's driving their need to kill to a fevered pitch? Or are they simply becoming bolder, becoming more confident that they won't get caught? Or do they want to get caught? Sometimes serial killers reach a point in their sprees where they crave recognition for their kills. But really, what do I know? I'm not a profiler, not really. I'm an empath who simply has a ton of experience dealing with serial killers. Which ... seriously Sam? That's exactly what you need to use ... your empath abilities.

Keeping my eyes firmly shut, I addressed Nixon. "You need to drop your void shield or get the hell out of this room. I don't care which, but it needs to happen now." With each day, my control and strength over my abilities grew, but I still didn't possess the skill to push through or around Nixon's void ability like Austin could.

Grumbling under his breath, Nixon complied, and I went to work. I stretched out my consciousness, searching for a familiar darkness, one akin to what I'd felt within Malcolm. It wasn't long before I locked onto the inky blackness of the killer, but I had also learned from my dealings with Malcolm to keep somewhat of a distance, to slip into his mind and emotions only so far. Otherwise, I didn't know if I could handle the repercussions ... yet. I shuddered at the brief memory of what happened when I didn't heed that piece of information before, or rather hadn't known any better.

I dragged my nails down my skin. "Please. Please help me." I'm contaminated. I need to get it off before it's too late. Before it kills me.

"He's on his way, Samantha. Hang on."

"Make it stop!" I screamed, tearing at my skin. "Please make it stop!" The dark poison seeped from every pore, every organ, slowly killing me. It's already too late. "Make it stop!"

Being inside of Malcolm's demented mind had made me feel contaminated, quite literally. And Austin, as usual, had helped me to sort through the taint infecting me. But this time—this time if I screwed up, I was on my own. *It doesn't matter. I've come such a long way, and I can, and will, do what needs to be done. I have to. Austin is depending on me.*

"Pay attention, Nixon," I murmured. "I'm about to link up with our friendly neighborhood serial killer."

I was confident Nixon would indeed be taking notes, at least metaphorically. He hated Austin enough to arrange the perfect circumstances for his death, but in the end, he was more dedicated to his job.

Opening my mind just a bit more, I let the dark emotions of the serial killer trickle into my consciousness. "He didn't want any of this. He wanted them, to be close to them, to touch them, but what he's become ruined everything, and yet he craves more. He wanted to be as close as possible, to feel what they feel, and he can't imagine anything better than being inside of them while they die, both physically and ... and—"

The sudden realization caused shock to zing through my system, and I mentally recoiled, my eyes snapping open. My gaze met Nixon's. "He's an empath, too."

He blinked rapidly as if my words were taking time to process. "H-How is that even possible?" he finally managed.

I jumped to my feet and began to pace the small space in front of my bed. "I don't know. But I know what I picked up on just now. And he's an empath. I'm one hundred percent sure."

Glancing at Nixon, I registered the slight edge of panic bleeding into his dark brown eyes. My heart quadrupled in time as I let the implications of my discovery truly wash over me. "Maybe it's inevitable that strong empaths find their way to death's addiction."

The question had cycled through my mind on an endless loop recently, whether or not I was capable of killing someone to fulfill my dark cravings. At the moment, the answer was no … but what if it changed? What if I one day lost myself completely to the addiction of feeling death?

The corners of my eyes burned, and a lump formed in my throat. "I don't want to be like that, Nixon. I can't—I just can't."

Austin. I need you right now. Only you can truly understand what I'm going through.

Nixon was on his feet and taking my trembling body into his arms a moment later. "I won't let that happen. Never. I'll never let that happen."

Barking out a laugh, I pulled away from him. "Hasn't anyone ever told you to never say never?" A humorless smile curled my lips as I met his gaze steadily. "There's no way anyone can guarantee that I won't turn into that. I thought what happened to Maggie, Malcolm, and me, was because of our line of work, but now …" I shook my head slowly. "Now I'm not so sure. I mean, seriously … What are the chances that this serial killer just so happens to be an empath, too? It's not a coincidence. It can't be. There's a connection, and the only one I can see is the whole empath thing."

Nixon's jaw muscle jumped as he stared me down with fierce determination. I could already see his wheels turning. "You don't know that yet. We need to track him down and find out more. You were drawn to him for a reason, maybe there's more here that will help you."

"Yeah, maybe." But I didn't believe my own words. I desperately wanted to, but I knew better than to hold onto false hope when there was none to be found.

Nixon snapped his fingers. "Sam, focus. Did you get a feel for where he might be? Anything at all that might help us track him?"

"No, I didn't stay linked to him for long. I'm going to have to go back in to find out more."

"All right, so let's do that." Nixon inched closer to me, reaching out a hand to touch my arm tentatively. "We'll figure this out—together."

My nostrils flared as I sucked in a ragged breath. It took an astronomical amount of willpower not to jerk away from his touch. There was no *together* for us anymore, and Nixon needed to come to terms with that reality. But I also currently needed his help if I had any real shot at saving Austin.

"All right," I murmured. "I'll go back in, but I want to center myself first." My eyes darted wildly around the hotel room in search of an excuse to put some temporary distance between us. There was only one feasible option. "I'm going to take a shower. I'll be out in a few." I slipped past Nixon without another word.

Once I was safely inside the bathroom with the door locked, I slumped against the wall, trembling. *I hope you're doing better than I am wherever you are, Austin. Just hang on. Because I'm going to fix this—all of it. Somehow. Even if I have to face my deepest fears head-on without a safety net. I will do anything to save you. Anything.*

Chapter 11

My heart thudded dully in my chest as I stared up at the bright yellow house with white shutters. It stood tall and bright, exuding a false cheeriness into the world, the dark torrent of emotions inside completely camouflaged to anyone without abilities like mine.

I glanced over at Nixon who was in the driver's seat of our SUV. "And to think the whole time we were 'married'," I raised my hands to form air quotes, "I thought you had no control over your void ability. Guess you lied about that, too."

Of course I'd recovered my memories with the knowledge of what he could and couldn't do, but I was in the mood to jab at him a bit.

Nixon dipped his head for a moment before focusing his chocolate eyes back on me intently. "Yeah, well, I did what I needed to do to protect you."

I snorted. "Protect your lies, you mean. Wasn't it exhausting?"

He heaved a huge sigh, focusing his attention on the yellow house. "You sure this is the place?" he asked, effectively changing the subject.

"Yep. Creepy, isn't it?"

Nixon nodded, his gaze still fixated on the house. "Yeah, it really is."

"I wonder if he's going to be like his house? All smiles and good manners on the outside and—"

"Patrick Bateman on the inside?"

I chuckled despite myself. "Technically, that's exactly how Patrick Bateman was though … perfect on the outside and crazy on the inside." I unhooked my seatbelt and pushed my door open. "Well, only one way to find out." I sent up a silent prayer that our friendly neighborhood serial killer would have the answers I needed.

Nixon fell into step beside me as we approached the house in silence. This was the first time I'd ever simply walked up to a serial killer's house and knocked on their front door. There wasn't exactly protocol in place for such a situation, or even any helpful tips.

I lifted my hand to push the doorbell, but Nixon grabbed my wrist. "Let me take the lead."

"I don't really see who rings the doorbell as making any kind of difference, but whatever."

Nixon tugged me behind him. *Oh, so he means take the lead literally, by standing in front of me.* Glaring at his back, I swallowed back the urge to argue about him taking his protectiveness a step too far as usual. It wasn't as if I was defenseless, after all. My mind was a weapon.

Abruptly, the door swung open, our person of interest looming in front of us. I choked back a gasp as an oppressive silence slammed into me. But it was more than mere silence. I heard something within it—because even nothing is something. And that lack of sound sucked me under, turning my world upside down … again.

An image of a boy in a hospital bed peering up at me superimposed itself over the adult man standing in the doorway. The two shared the same mousy brown hair, luminous green eyes, pale skin, and sharp features. Shock zinged through my system, my heart taking off at a gallop. The serial killer was the boy all grown up. They were one and the same. And I knew him. Somehow, I'd met him before.

But how? All my memories were returned to me, and yet I still had no recollection of any time in a hospital as a kid. Despite that fact, I knew with complete certainty that I knew this man, and I had met him when we were both children.

"Sam." Nixon's voice shattered the nothing that was entombing my senses, and I shook my head, disbelief still holding me in place.

The killer's eyes widened as he stared at me, finally blurting, "I know you." His level of surprise matched mine.

"Yes," I whispered.

Staggering back, he clutched at his throat and crumpled to the ground in a heap. Instinctively, I dove into his mind without even a moment's hesitation.

He couldn't breathe. It was as if someone was sitting on his chest and choking him at the same time. His heart thundered in his ears, his thoughts becoming erratic. An image of a woman, one that seemed familiar to me flashed in his mind's eye. But what was most surprising ... he'd been expecting his death. That knowledge, as he slipped away, robbed me of the satisfaction of sharing in his eminent demise. It was the same when I shared in the death of someone who'd been ill for a long period of time. It was like getting one bite of the cake you've been craving ... it only left you wanting more.

"Damn it," I muttered.

Nixon knelt beside the body. "He's dead."

I gritted my teeth. "Thanks, Captain Obvious."

Nixon slid in behind the body and hooked it under the arms, dragging it back into the house. "Coming?" He shot me a questioning look.

"Yeah ... yeah." I stepped inside, pulling the door shut behind me. Irritation sizzled through my veins, leaving my nerves exposed. I'd gotten a taste—just a mouthful of what I'd been craving—and I wanted ... needed more.

As Nixon stood, his gaze slid over me intently. "You didn't slip in to feel his death?"

"I did."

"Then why ..." He cleared his throat. "Then why aren't you—"

"In a state of euphoria?"

“Yeah.” Cupping the back of his neck, he turned away from me.

I snorted. “What? Were you hoping I’d get a little frisky afterwards?”

“Yeah, I guess I kind of was,” Nixon mumbled.

Laughter erupted from my chest, and I doubled over. The situation—the dead body, Nixon, just everything—was beyond ridiculous, and definitely not funny, which was why I couldn’t help but laugh.

Sobering a moment later, I grimaced at the ache in my side. “At least you’re finally being honest. What? You don’t mind me taking a trip into the dark and demented if it benefits you?” I raised my hand even though he wasn’t looking at me. “Wait. Don’t bother answering that, it was rhetorical. Good to know you’re just like the rest of us, though.”

Nixon cleared his throat. “Were you able to get anything from his mind?”

“He wasn’t surprised he was dying. That’s why I didn’t get the euphoric pop that I normally do from a sudden death like his. And he thought briefly about a woman that seemed familiar to me, although I can’t place her at the moment. And before that …”

The image of him as a child skidded across my brain again. “I know him. Or I did.” I suddenly wanted to punch something. “Damn it, Nixon! It’s happening again. Why the fuck is it happening again?”

Nixon swung around to face me. “What’s happening again?”

"Me recalling memories that shouldn't exist," I ground out between clenched teeth. "I knew him, but I don't know how. I saw an image of him in a hospital bed next to mine." I shook my head slowly, trying to dislodge my confusion. "I was never in a hospital when I was a kid, Nixon. At least not that I remember. So, you see, it's happening again."

"Show me what you saw."

"Oh, yeah, that's right, you can pull back your void shield whenever you feel like it. Since you kept that little detail hidden from me during our fake marriage, I keep forgetting."

"Sam," Nixon snapped. "This is—"

"Bigger than us. Yeah, I know." But just because I was forced to work with Nixon under the current circumstances didn't mean I'd keep my mouth shut. He needed to be reminded that our marriage had been a lie and that I loved Austin and not him.

Shooting daggers at him with my eyes, I stepped into him and lifted my hand to press my fingertips into his temple. I didn't need to do that when I was at the top of my game, but I was a bit frazzled, and skin-to-skin contact made it easier. I quickly replayed the memory and the image of the woman I'd snagged from the killer's mind as he died.

"Fuck." Nixon reared back from me and tugged at his hair, grimacing. "That was Maggie. You saw Maggie."

"Maggie?" Before her name finished leaving my mouth the memory slammed into me.

A dim apartment, Malcolm cradling a petite brunette in his arms, tears streaking down his cheeks. Austin stood a few feet away, hunched over. Tension, guilt, and sadness twisted his face into one I almost didn't recognize.

"I'm sorry, Malcolm. So sorry. More than you'll ever know. But it had to be done. You have to know it had to be done."

A broken sob escaped Malcolm. "Why? Why would you do this to me?"

Austin flicked his gaze away as his shoulders sagged. "You know why."

"I love her! You know I love her! How could you do this to me?" Malcolm screamed, spittle flying from his mouth.

"You screwed up. You fell in too deep. You'll get over it and realize what you felt wasn't really love. She had to die. You know she had to die."

"No! I love her!" Malcolm couldn't tear his eyes from the small woman in his arms. "Maggie. Please. I love you. Maggie ..." Her name rolled off his tongue with reverence, devotion, and clear and unconditional love. "I need her. Please, I need her."

IT WASN'T MY MEMORY, but one that Malcolm had shown me. Maggie was the woman he loved—the one that Austin eliminated under direct orders because she'd begun killing for enjoyment. Just like Malcolm had in the end. And also just like the freshly dead empath had. Three empaths, all with death addictions, and all of them connected. But how? None of it made any sense now that the third empath had been added to the equation.

I swore under my breath. "It's all connected somehow. All of it."

"Yeah, it is, but I don't fucking have a clue how." Nixon's gaze darted around our surroundings as he assessed what the next step should be. "We need to search the house and snag whatever information we can. I have a feeling we don't have much time."

He moved towards the stairs on his right. "I'll take upstairs." He nodded in the direction of the kitchen. "You start down here." He made it up a couple of steps before he paused. "And don't eat or drink anything. I think he was poisoned."

"No shit," I mumbled, pivoting on my heels. It wasn't my first time at the rodeo, and I wasn't a complete idiot. *Of course,* what's-his-name had probably been poisoned and the timing was impeccable, too. It was just another item to add to the list of things I needed answers to ... Who knew we'd be coming and decided to take out our only source of information?

As I began searching the dead empath's house, I couldn't shake the feeling that I was being manipulated and steered towards something. And I had no choice but to comply since I'd once again been thrust into a game where I didn't know the rules or even the players.

Chapter 12

"You need to tell me more about Natalie and her operation, and while you're at it you need to tell me about David and his operation. I've known way too little for too long and that's all about to change."

Nixon sighed heavily, his knuckles turning white as he gripped the steering wheel. "What do you want to know?"

"Everything," I grated. "But how about we start with the part of who is Natalie … exactly? And David, who is—was he? And what about the part of how it seemed so easy for us to move from one operation to the other and back again, as if they were interchangeable. I've been accepting half-ass explanations for things for way too long just because I thought I was helping people, saving lives, but nothing is what I thought, is it?"

"I don't have all the answers you want, Sam. But I'm going to do my best. I'll tell you everything I know."

"All right." I crossed my arms over my chest, staring at him expectantly.

A car honked, speeding past us, and Nixon accelerated, completely unflustered.

Nixon tapped his thumbs rapidly on the steering wheel, before white-knuckling it again. "Okay," he grated, his jaw muscles feathering, "Natalie and David used to be married."

Whaaat? Of all the things he could have said there was a zero percent chance I would have ever guessed that.

"From what I understand, for a time, everyone was one big, happy family working for the US government. But then Natalie and David had a falling out over something. I'm not sure about what, although it was enough to not only break up the team but their marriage."

Nixon glanced over at me where I remained frozen and speechless in shock. "They came to an agreement or arrangement, if you will. Natalie could keep doing what she did, if she didn't get in David's way. And as payment for her not getting in his way, he would pretend like we didn't exist. It was acceptable terms for both of them."

"So, when you took me and ran ..."

"Yep, there was nothing Natalie could do about it. I knew going to David would be my only course of action to keep you safe."

"But Malcolm worked for the government, too. How many branches of people like us are out there?" The more answers I got the more questions I had.

"I told you I don't have all the answers, Sam. I'm

beginning to think all of us have been kept in the dark about these things for a reason. And I'm also beginning to think we're all pawns in a much bigger game."

I nibbled on my bottom lip. "That's exactly what I was thinking before. So you see, you have to let Austin go. You have to—"

"No. Just because we don't have all the answers doesn't change things with Austin. I'm still in charge, and I'm going to run things the way I see fit now. And if Austin is responsible for—"

"He's not!" I screeched. My entire body shook with the amount of effort it took to keep me from completely exploding. I punched the dashboard, the sharp sting reverberating up my arm and centering me. "And how exactly did you end up in charge again? Maybe you're the one who made Natalie *disappear*."

Either unaffected or not noticing my rage, Nixon snorted. "You really think I'd do that, to what … get Austin out of the way?"

Digging my nails into my palms, I leaned closer to him. "Actually, yeah, I do. I'm beginning to realize that you're capable of a lot more than I ever thought possible." Nixon tensed and I chuckled, the sound bitter even to my ears. "After all, you did hijack my life and pretend to be my husband."

Nixon's spine went ramrod straight, his breaths shallow, as he accelerated past a truck, the SUV shaking slightly. I waited for some kind of a response, even if it was pointless. Because we both knew there was nothing he could say in his defense that would sound good in any way. He'd swiped my memories, essentially brainwashing me into becoming the woman he'd claimed as his wife. For two entire years I'd lived my life as someone who didn't exist, and there was no coming back from that kind of betrayal.

Anger and guilt churned in my gut, mixing to form a special kind of hatred for Nixon. All those times he held me, told me he loved me—every single time he pushed into me, and I accepted him into my body, convinced he was the man I wanted—loved, all because of his lies and manipulations. No, there was nothing he could ever say to make me forgive him for what he'd done to me, and Austin for that matter.

"I found a list of names," Nixon blurted, reaching into his pocket and pulling a folded piece of paper out. He shoved it in my direction.

Snatching it from him, I raised my eyebrows as I unfolded the paper. "And?"

"And … my name is on the list. My real name."

Scanning said list, I noted it was a printout of an Exel Document. "But how is that possible? Your real name was erased from everyone's mind except yours, and I guess Austin's since he did the majority of the erasing. Was there someone before him that—"

The rest of my question stuck in my throat as my eyes came to rest on the name: *Chloe Ransic*. My name was on the list, too. I didn't know what Nixon's name had once been, but I knew Austin's, at least his first name. My eyes darted down the page, snagging on an Alex. I couldn't be one hundred percent certain that the Alex on the list was Austin, but since both Nixon and me were on it, I would have put money down that it was him. "I don't understand. What does this mean?"

"Your name is also on the list then? I had my suspicions."

"Mine and Austin's both."

"He told you his real name?" he choked out, as if he was surprised. But why would he be? Or maybe it was simply because Nixon had never shared his with me and he couldn't wrap his mind around Austin doing what he never could. Of course, all Nixon ever shared with me was lies heaped upon more lies. The intimacy of such truths obviously didn't come easy to him.

I shrugged. "He told me his first name at least. Why? Does that mean something to you?" Perhaps Nixon still doubted Austin's love for me and I needed to work on proving it to him in order to save Austin's life.

"No. Nothing. It means nothing to me," Nixon snapped.

A few heartbeats of silence passed before he cleared his throat. "So all of our names are on some printout that another serial killer empath had in his office. The same serial killer that had memories of Maggie and also of you as a child. And then that same serial killer conveniently dies minutes after we arrive to see him from apparent poisoning. What. The. Fuck?"

"My sentiments exactly," I muttered. "We have to do something. I mean, we can't just ignore this."

The SUV swerved across two lanes of traffic, skidding to a stop on the side of the road. Before I had time to react, Nixon palmed the back of my neck, his familiar chocolate gaze boring into mine. "I know what you're doing, and I gave you your chance. These questions may need answered, but they have nothing to do with Natalie and Austin and the rest of that mess. I—"

I flung his hand away from me. "I'm not trying to hide my motivations from you. I'm trying to save the life of the man I love. The man who has been wrongly accused of things you know he would never do."

Nixon reached for me again, and I slapped him across the face. He reared back and grimaced.

"What? You think I'm holding on to some kind of tenderness for you? You think we'll pick up our relationship where we left off if Austin's out of the way?"

My palm connected with his jaw again. "No. I don't love you. I never loved you. How many times do you need to be told that?" My anger dissolved into despair when I considered that there was a very real possibility that I would never be in Austin's arms again. Never hear his voice again. Never—

Choking back a sob, I bit my hand. "I'll kill you."

Nixon leaned away from me, stunned.

"That's right. If he's put to death because of you, I'll kill you."

Digging my nails into the console, I curled my lips

away from my teeth, letting the darkness that lived inside of me peer out. "I'll kill you with my bare hands and I'll enjoy every last second of it because you would be the one responsible for taking away the person who means the most in the world to me."

Nixon's eyes cooled as he stared at me. "Are you threatening me, Sam?"

"No. I'm making you a promise. If you cause Austin's death, you *will* pay with your life."

Something sharp was thrust into my thigh and I jumped. Glancing down, I spotted a syringe protruding from my jeans. "You mother fucker," I hissed as I yanked the needle out and chucked it in Nixon's direction. "I can't believe you drugged—"

My head swam and my vision blurred just as all my thoughts slipped away into nothingness.

Chapter 13

My lips twitched up into a smile as I gazed down at my blindfolded and tethered husband. Even in his seemingly vulnerable position, he was still very much in control. He was letting me play with him—I knew it and he knew that I knew it—but it was still fun to pretend otherwise.

Climbing onto the bed, I situated myself next to him and ran my hands slowly over his well-defined body from his chest down to his abs. I danced my fingertips along his hips, resisting the urge to go lower. He remained perfectly still in blatant defiance. But I was determined to make him squirm. Dipping my head, I followed the path my hands had just traveled with my tongue—not even a muscle twitched.

He's really going to make me work for this. Asshole.

Groaning in frustration, I skimmed my teeth over his abs and then nipped. And still, he remained perfectly relaxed. "Why do I feel like you're topping me from the bottom?"

Austin's lips curled up slightly at the corners.

"You promised you'd give me a turn, Austin." I fought to keep the whine out of my voice. Dominant women simply did not do that. I was dominant in almost every scenario except when I was having sex with Austin. Then I had a tendency to give myself completely to him and his whims. Not that I was complaining, but I wanted to own his body in the way he owned mine.

"You have to make me submit to you," Austin said gruffly.

All right, if he wanted me to step up my game then I would. I slid his cock into my mouth, sucking hard. His hips lifted off the bed slightly and I knew I was on the right track. Guess I just have to go for it instead of teasing.

I moved up and down on his length as I circled and flicked him with my tongue. Soon I added my hand to the mix with a little twisting motion that made Austin groan low in the back of his throat. I immediately pulled away from him. My new goal was to make him beg. I smiled as he shifted his hips impatiently in a silent plea for me to continue my ministrations.

I waited a few moments before straddling his hips and pressing my naked breasts against his chest. Leaning forward, I whispered in his ear, "I'm going to make you beg me for it."

His breath caught in his throat, and I couldn't help the grin that spread across my face. I was definitely starting to enjoy myself.

Pressing my hot, wet core against the tip of his cock, I held him there, not letting him go any farther as I nibbled and kissed his neck, continuing to tease. Finally, when I couldn't take it anymore,

I pushed myself down onto him roughly, a deep groan escaping his parted lips. I tried to keep my pace slow and steady—tortuous as I dragged it out—but my own impatience won as I slammed onto him faster and faster. My muscles coiled tight, and I fell over the edge, golden flecks dancing behind closed lids as I moaned. A few seconds later Austin spasmed within me, following suit.

My breaths were still erratic as I slid the blindfold off of his beautiful baby blues, staring deeply into them as they blinked lazily at me. A devilish grin stretched his full lips. "I think it's my turn again."

Abruptly, I found myself on my back with my arms pinned above my head. "Hey!" I wriggled in protest. "How did you get out of those ropes?"

Shaking his head slowly, he chuckled as delight curled his lips. "Ah, Sammy, Sammy, Sammy ... my good Sammy girl, did you really think you could keep me tied up if I didn't want to be?"

"You're such an asshole, Austin! Let me go! You promised I could be in control tonight!"

Me struggling against him only made his grin widen. "And I changed my mind." He pressed into me. "Just give me a few minutes and I'll be good to go again." He took my mouth forcefully, sliding his tongue in to intertwine with mine.

I stopped fighting him, my objections nullified by lust. I idly wondered if that's how it'd always be with him.

"Only with me, Sam. Remember that. I'm the only one who could ever truly dominate you—because you let me. What we have is different," Austin's voice whispered in my mind as I

began slowly returning to consciousness. *"Don't let anyone control you. Do what you need to do."*

It was just a dream memory. Austin's not really with me. My heart twisted in anguish as I made that realization.

Wait. Nixon drugged me. The conversation we had just before I'd been forced into unconsciousness came flooding back, and I knew Austin was making a point, using the memory as a precursor to his message to hit it home. Even though it wasn't the same as having him physically with me, I still rejoiced that he was able to make contact with me mentally. Something that maybe would have seemed insignificant to someone, anyone else, helped more than I could put into words. Since I'd been separated from Austin, yet again, there'd been an emptiness growing inside of me created by his absence. *I need you, Austin.*

Listening intently, I heard nothing but the hum of an engine, and the sound of other cars whizzing by. I slitted my eyes open, seeing the back of the passenger seat directly in front of me. Nixon obviously put me in the back seat of the SUV once he'd drugged me. If Nixon was still driving, then I hadn't been unconscious for that long.

I quickly closed my eyes again and peered out from behind my lashes, just in case Nixon decided to check on me. *But now what?* I couldn't attack Nixon because then we might crash, and there was the fact that he was now in charge—what would happen to Austin if Nixon was injured? Would Austin be blamed therefore leading to his death sentence being carried out? Or perhaps Nixon's death would ultimately lead to Austin's release since I might have a better shot at someone who would actually listen to the evidence of my husband's innocence?

"I know you're awake," Nixon stated blandly. "So no use pretending."

Heaving a sigh, I sat up, shooting the back of Nixon's head with my best death glare. "What was the point of all of that if I didn't even stay unconscious for the rest of the trip? Seems like an effort in futility if you ask me."

"I didn't ask you."

"Okaaay," I grated. "So what do you plan on doing with me then?" I really wished I could use my offensive abilities on him. *Damn void powers.*

"That dose should have kept you under for at least five or six more hours if you must know."

I raised my eyebrows and slouched back into the cool leather. "How'd you know I was awake then, and how am I at all for that matter?"

"I suspect Austin," Nixon spat.

Sometimes it was surreal to think that Austin and Nixon used to be friends. Now they held nothing but contempt for each other and I was the one to blame. *Just call me Yoko.*

"Interesting." So Nixon thought Austin had somehow gotten past his void powers to give my mind a little wake-up call? And somehow he'd also helped me fight the effects of the drug as well? Huh. I wouldn't have believed it, but I knew Austin was getting more powerful, and we did share a special connection. I guessed the dream memory served as a sort of confirmation, but I wasn't about to tell Nixon anything that wasn't absolutely necessary.

"I can tell by your expression you know it was Austin," Nixon said, snapping me out of my inner musings.

I scowled. Nixon had grown very good at reading me in the years we were fake married. "Yeah, okay, maybe it was ... so I'll ask again—what are you planning on doing with me?"

"We're heading to Pittsburgh."

What?

"Pittsburgh? Why Pittsburgh?" I hadn't been back to my hometown since I'd gone undercover at the strip club I used to bartend at to hunt down a serial killer.

I studied Nixon's expressionless face in the rearview mirror. "Well, when you were out, I decided to check on a few of the other names on that list. I'm not sure if they're still there, but two of them are supposedly living in Pittsburgh."

I snorted. "Of course. Everything keeps leading me back there for some reason."

"Yeah, and I don't think that's a coincidence."

AS THE LIGHTS of downtown Pittsburgh glowed on the horizon, slowly coming into view, I mumbled, "Welcome to Shittsburgh."

It was a bit discombobulating to hate a place with such

raw ferocity while still considering it home. It wasn't Steel City's fault though. It was merely the unlucky location where a ton of bullshit had gone down in my life. Especially recently.

I was forced to return to my hometown and go undercover as a stripper when tracking the serial killer who Malcolm was controlling. I was also having a major identity crisis at the time since all of my real memories had been stolen from me. But I was born and raised in Pittsburgh, and despite the bad associations, the city had shaped who I was as a person. For better or worse, it would always be a part of me.

As we continued to drive, headed for the Squirrel Hill Tunnels, my gaze narrowed on the back of Nixon's head. What would have happened if Malcom had never resurfaced to stir up the real memories of my past? Would Austin have eventually found me? Or would I have lived out the rest of my life thinking Nixon was my husband? I shuddered at the thought.

Although I'd been having dreams and fantasies about Austin … there was a possibility that Dr. Gray might have been able to convince me to push them aside. Or perhaps in the end I would have left Nixon? And how would he have prevented that outcome if I was unhappy in our marriage?

But beyond all of that, the question I kept coming back to was why exactly did Nixon love me to the point of obsession? I cheated on and left him for Austin. In fact, when presented with the option, I'd chosen Austin over him every single time. Why didn't he move the fuck on like a normal person? If I could convince him to finally let go of the idea of being with me, then maybe he'd simply release Austin.

I sucked on my teeth before heaving a huge sigh. Nixon sat up straighter in his seat. He knew I was about to break the silence and he was waiting to hear what I had to say.

"Why do you love me, Nixon?"

A few moments ticked by before he responded. "Of all the things I thought you might say ..." He barked out a humorless laugh. "That was not even a possibility in my mind."

"Do you even know?" I persisted.

"Tell me why you love Austin," he retorted.

Normally I wouldn't dignify his question with a response, but I knew I was going to have to play along with him if I had any hope of getting legitimate answers out of him. "I love him because I—"

"Don't bullshit me, Sam. You can't answer that question any more than I can about you. The heart wants what the heart wants, and sometimes we don't get much of a say in it."

Damn him for throwing my words back at me.

Leaning back in my seat, I crossed my arms. "Yeah, well ... you shouldn't. Love me that is. I haven't exactly treated you good, have I? In fact, I don't even know how you stand to be around me at all after everything I've done to you."

"Austin hasn't treated you good and you still love him."

"Not true. Austin just has a bit of an ego. That doesn't mean he's treated me badly. To start with, he's never cheated on me."

Nixon snorted. "That you know of."

"No, he hasn't cheated. He hasn't been with anyone but me since we've been officially together."

"What about when he thought you were dead?"

Here we go again. I ground my teeth together. Nixon brought up that point several times already, hoping to get to me. But I refused to let him use his knowledge of my insecurities to play Austin and me against each other.

I met his gaze in the rearview mirror as I notched my chin up. "It doesn't matter because him thinking I was dead is an extenuating circumstance."

"So you're going to sit there and tell me that you don't care if he fucked dozens of women when the two of you were apart?" Nixon's voice held a note of incredulousness.

Dozens? No, don't think about it. Don't let Nixon get to you. "I won't lie. I care. But I won't let it get to me. After all, I was fucking you the entire time."

"I can't believe I'm going to say this," Nixon mumbled under his breath before he said louder for my benefit, "It's not the same. You didn't have your real memories. Nothing you did with me could be held against you. If he—"

"If he fucked hundreds of girls, I'd still forgive him. He thought I was dead. And it would have been just sex. He loves me. Grief does weird things to people." I was rationalizing, but it didn't make it any less true. Austin didn't cheat on me. He thought I was dead. And I had absolutely no clue if he did have sex with anyone during our time apart. Although I was guessing he had.

"If it'd been me and I thought you were dead, I wouldn't have so much as looked at anyone else. Maybe ever again," Nixon said softly.

"This isn't about you!" I punched the back of his headrest. "I love Austin. He is who he is, and I accept that." Settling back in my seat, I snorted. "And I don't believe you."

Nixon was silent for what seemed like an eternity before he finally spoke again. "Since our first time together … I haven't been with anyone but you."

Shock rippled through me. "But I thought—"

"You thought wrong."

I chewed on my bottom lip as I studied Nixon's face in the side mirror. Before he stole me away to play my faux husband, I thought he'd been with a few women. But the fact that he hadn't been with anyone else but me—hadn't wanted to be—well shit.

My heart fisted with … Sympathy? Pity? Admiration? I wasn't sure. But his words meant something to me. Not that I would ever choose Nixon over Austin. Not that I would ever choose anyone over Austin. I simply wished I could say with one hundred percent certainty that Austin hadn't been with hundreds of women when he thought I was dead—that he was wired in that one aspect like

Nixon. *It doesn't matter. It's different with me and Austin. He loves me.*

Am I enough though? Some guys can compartmentalize sex and love—keep them separate. *No.* I shook my head to dislodge those thoughts. I wouldn't let Nixon drudge up old insecurities in me. When I said yes to Austin's marriage proposal, I also said yes to him as he was … to trusting that his love for me was enough, that our love was enough.

I drummed my nails along my jean-clad thigh. "Never mind. I shouldn't have asked you that question. It was bad judgment on my part."

"You just don't want to face the truth about him."

Nixon was baiting me, but I couldn't seem to resist. "And what would this so-called truth be?"

"That you love Austin more than he loves you, if he even really knows what love is."

My nostrils flared and I ground my teeth together, barely holding my fury in check. I had two choices. One: I could let myself be drawn into the fight Nixon was clearly trying to pick with me about Austin. Or two: I could not even bother to dignify him with a response and ignore him until we reached our destination.

Much to Nixon's dismay, I chose option number two.

Chapter 14

"And who exactly lives here?" I asked the back of Nixon's head as I glared at it. Fighting the urge to pull out a clump of his hair, my hands curled into fists. *You can do this. Remain civil. Or at the very least don't physically accost him.*

He steered the SUV into the steeply sloped driveway of a small, dingy house in Turtle Creek, PA, which was about twenty minutes from downtown Pittsburgh.

Nixon yanked on the emergency break and glanced up at the house number before referring to a piece of paper he withdrew from his pocket. "A Mr. Jason Scott."

I scooted over to the left side door, peering up at the house through the window. "Why'd you pick his name off the list first?"

Nixon shrugged. "It was the easiest location to get to of the Pittsburgh people."

It was as good a reason as any. "Okay, so what's the

plan?" Because of course Nixon would have a fully fleshed out plan before doing anything. He would never fly by the seat of his pants like I usually found myself doing.

Ignoring my question, Nixon slid out of the SUV smoothly and made his way up the front walk, not bothering to wait for me. *Asshole.*

I hopped out the back door, sprinting to catch up with him. "How about dropping your void wall? I'd like to be able to use my empath skills."

Nixon gave me a sidelong glance and kept walking. "I don't want him to get a read on us if he has abilities, too. We don't know what we're dealing with yet."

"Getting no read is still something if he's an empath. He's going to know something's up."

"The best offense is a good defense," Nixon said smoothly.

I growled under my breath. I'd been 'married' to him long enough to know when I was fighting a losing battle. Now was one of those times. He'd made up his mind and nothing I could say or do would change it.

"So what are we going to do, just ring the bell?"

He still hadn't filled me in on his plan, if he even had one. Maybe he actually didn't for the first time in history and he simply didn't want to admit it to me of all people.

"Basically."

I tried to stifle a laugh ... unsuccessfully. The sharp sound erupted from me as I sputtered out, "It sounds like a plan I would come up with." Which translated to no plan according to him.

Nixon's left eye twitched. "No, it doesn't."

Our conversation halted as we reached the door and Nixon pushed the doorbell, the chimes echoing inside. We waited in tense silence for what seemed like an eternity before he rang the bell again. When no sounds came from within, Nixon reached up to knock, but as soon as his knuckles made contact with the faded and cracked black paint, it creaked open. He glanced at me with a mixture of wariness and surprise.

"That's not suspicious or anything," I whispered.

"Or something straight out of a movie," Nixon said dryly.

"Do you think we should just go in?" I wanted to, but also didn't relish the idea of walking in to find a gun pointed at my face or something as equally unsavory.

Nixon exhaled loudly through his nose. "I'm going to drop my void shield to let you see if you pick up on anything."

I smiled tightly, anticipation elevating my heart rate. "About time." I chose to ignore the look of annoyance Nixon speared me with.

I'm so cold. And there's so much blood. It's kind of weird looking—almost like it's fake. But I know it's not. I used to think about death a lot when I was younger, was afraid of what it would be like to feel my own, and now here I am. I suppose it's karma, after all, I've taken so many people's lives before their time. But I didn't want to ... not really. I just wanted to—

I knew you'd come. Better hurry before I'm dead.

I gasped as I blinked Nixon back into view. The person

whose mind I'd just been in, he felt my presence within his mind and was communicating with me.

Shoving the door open, I ran headlong into the house. Whoever was inside was another empath … another empath who was dying just as we arrived. And I needed answers before there was no one alive to give them.

"Sam!" Nixon called after me, but I ignored him. Although it didn't really matter, I knew he would follow me.

My gaze darted around the interior of the small house, almost immediately alighting on the crumpled body lying in a pool of blood a few feet to the right. I rushed forward and dropped to my knees, paying the sticky red liquid no mind.

"I knew you'd come." The man … the empath's eyes fluttered open, his unfocused gaze attempting to find mine. He sucked in a ragged breath, the sound wet and painful. His dark skin, already ashen, was growing paler by the second. "I should have listened but I thought you … *were paranoid*." He finished in my mind, obviously losing the battle with his dying body.

"What are you talking about?" I demanded. "How did you know I was coming?"

His mind attempted to push at mine, but he was too weak. Unable to resist staying away from his death any longer, I slipped into his instead.

He was surprised. He hadn't been expecting me, but … the image of the serial killer from Ohio was conjured up for me to see. Then his emotions turned to regret—regret for not listening, for not wanting to believe. He wasn't ready to die, and yet it was too late—too late for anything. I heard myself laugh with joy. Regret was the sweetest dying emotion of them all. He regretted, and I would thrive. His mind was growing dimmer, but I continued to focus on his regret as it morphed into euphoria within me. As his last breath escaped his lungs, I expanded my chest with oxygen effortlessly. I laughed again.

"*Sam, need you here,*" Austin whispered into my mind as if from a distance, his voice barely audible. "*Felt it all with you.*"

Shock was quickly replaced with my own burning need. I wanted to take Austin inside of me like after the blast—to join our hearts, bodies, and souls in the celebration of living after experiencing death together.

"Austin." I brushed my hands along my sensitive body, something warm and sticky sliding over my exposed skin.

"Sam." Strong arms wrapped around me, lifting. "Jesus fucking Christ."

"I need you, too, Austin," I murmured, pressing my sticky hands against the hard chest that I was cradled against.

"Sam, you need to snap out of it and open your goddamn eyes," the same familiar voice demanded.

Not that I cared.

"No. I need you now." My body was thrumming with the demand to be touched. But no one seemed to be obliging me, and therefore I was becoming increasingly desperate. "Please," I croaked out as I caressed my hard nipples, shivering at the contact. "I need you, I need you so much."

Austin, along with all of his emotions, was suddenly ripped away from me, but it was too late. I'd felt the death and was lost in the afterglow. I writhed and moaned, running my hands along my curves, not stopping even when I was dropped onto some kind of soft surface with pillows.

"Not that you understand a damn word I'm saying right now, but I'm going to take a look around before we leave."

"Mmmm ..." I moaned, arching my back. With my eyes still closed, I imagined Austin's callused hands touching me instead of my own.

"That's what I thought," the voice said with a mixture of disgust and annoyance.

I slipped my hand into my pants, circling my clit just the way Austin would. It took almost no effort at all before I was screaming out my release, but it wasn't enough. I had to have more. I needed to revel in the feeling of being alive—and for that I needed sex.

My fingers fumbled with the buttons on my pants, and just as I managed to shimmy them about halfway down my thighs, I met resistance.

"No. You need to snap out of this. Sam, please."

It was the guttural sob that finally broke through my death-induced haze.

My eyes fluttered open, and I took in my situation with mounting horror. I was spread out on a paisley-patterned couch with several mismatched throw pillows scattered around me. My pants were shoved halfway down my thighs, and I was covered in blood. Most of it was already dry, but some of it still glistened on my skin.

Lifting my gaze to Nixon's, I watched as he blinked back tears as he stared down at me. It was there in the reflection of his limpid pools that I saw myself clearly.

"Oh God." I shuddered in revulsion, tears of my own flooding my eyes and obscuring his features behind a wall of watercolors.

What have I become?

I brought myself to orgasm while covered in the blood of someone whose body hadn't even cooled yet.

I'm a fucking monster.

Nausea roiled my gut, and bile shot up my esophagus. Convulsing, I doubled over to empty the contents of my stomach. My mind couldn't cope with the reality of what I'd done. Darkness pushed around the edges of my vision, and I welcomed the protection of the oblivion I fell into.

"SAMMY, MY GOOD SAMMY GIRL." *Austin's voice wrapped itself around me, warm and comforting.*

Whirling around, my excitement quickly turned to shock. Austin stood a few feet away from me. Naked ... and covered from head to toe in blood. It was as if he'd bathed in it. "Wh-What happened to you?"

He grinned, his teeth appearing even whiter in contrast to the red gore on his face. "It doesn't matter. Nothing matters but us."

He closed the scant distance between us, his hot breath skittering over my flesh, which was when I realized I was also naked. Only I didn't have so much as a drop of blood on me.

A high-pitched squeak escaped my throat as he dipped his head to kiss me. But as soon as his lips made contact, everything except Austin was forgotten. My body reacted as it always did for him—it immediately surrendered to his command.

His fingers trailed over my breasts, rolling my nipples. Goose bumps erupted across my skin, and I threw my head back when his mouth enclosed around one of the tight buds. He didn't linger long though, and soon he was making his way down my body, licking and sucking as he went. His first slow lick across my throbbing clit made my knees buckle, but Austin quickly reached around to support me. I gripped his hair tightly, holding him in place as I rocked my hips towards him. Only moments later my nervous system shattered into a million pieces and I moaned Austin's name.

"That's right. You know I'll always take care of you, Sammy. I love you so fucking much." Austin's voice was thick with love and lust, a beautiful combination.

Peering down at him as he tugged me towards the ground, shock surged through me. Blood—blood everywhere. We were both completely coated in it. How could I forget?

Despite the circumstances, I still didn't resist as Austin covered me with his body. As he entwined our hands, shifting above me, I turned my head to the right for some unknown reason—coming face to face with brown, lifeless eyes. I screamed as I bucked against Austin.

Tightening his grip on me, Austin murmured, "It'll be okay. Trust me, Sam, my good Sammy girl."

Unable to return my gaze to Austin's, I screamed again and again as I took in the horror of our surroundings. We were languishing amongst a sea of dead bodies. We were immersed in death, we were a part of it.

And suddenly the death emotions seeped into my consciousness just as Austin plunged into me, my screams morphing from terror to pleasure. I couldn't seem to help it. Nor did I want to deny myself the all-encompassing pleasure.

"Yes, Austin, yes!"

"Sam!" a familiar voice shouted in my ear. "Sam! Wake the fuck up!"

My eyes flew open, immediately focusing on Nixon's angst-ridden features. Throwing my arms around him, I buried my face in his neck. "Thank God!"

Even though we'd only been fake married, in that moment, being enfolded in his welcoming embrace was comforting. And I didn't care if he took my reaction to him the wrong way. I'd simply set him straight again later.

"For fuck's sake, Sam, what the hell just happened? You passed out and then I couldn't wake you up." The steel band of his arms tightened around me.

Shoving the residual images from my mind, I said, "Nightmare, all of it."

And I wasn't just talking about the dream, but what happened before with the empath and what had caused me to pass out to begin with. Shuddering, I shoved those memories aside as well. "We need to get out of here … we need to …"

Nixon pulled away, running his hands through my hair gently. "We're at a motel. You were passed out for a while which was why I was so worried."

"How did you get me here covered—"

"In blood?" Nixon sucked on his teeth. "I checked us in and then carried you in wrapped in a blanket. Although, this isn't the type of place where people talk, at least if you pay them not to, and I did."

"Oh."

"Tell me about your nightmare."

Standing slowly, my legs trembled beneath me, and I swayed as I let my gaze sweep the small room. Nixon hadn't been kidding. I was pretty sure the brown stain on the carpet was dried blood. In my current state, I fit right in. "I'm going to take a shower."

Nixon didn't say anything about me not answering his question, and he couldn't … not really. We weren't even pretending to be married anymore, so my secrets were mine and I didn't have to feel guilty about keeping them from him.

Once I was safely in the tiny and thoroughly disgusting bathroom, I stripped off my blood-encrusted clothes and tossed them in the corner to never think about again. I then turned on the shower as hot as it would go and stepped under the scorching spray. I was hoping I could clear my mind and rinse away the lingering disgust of myself.

As the pink-tinged water circled the drain, a plethora of questions sprang into my head. Who killed the two empaths just as Nixon and I arrived to see them? What did the list with all of our real names on it mean? And about the events surrounding Natalie's disappearance—why was the timeline off for everyone else? Plus, the nightmare … what did it mean exactly?

Those questions were just the tip of the iceberg though, and I needed to find the answers before the impending feeling of doom became more than impending. What I really needed was Austin with me and not Nixon. But first I had to convince Nixon that Austin wasn't guilty of any wrongdoing in regards to the blast.

I sighed with exasperation and thumped my head against the grimy shower wall. It was official … if this kind of drama happened every time I visited Pittsburgh, no matter how much I thought of it as home, I was done.

Chapter 15

"Who are we going after next on the list?" I demanded as soon as I stepped out of the bathroom.

"No—huh-uh. Not after what happened. We're going back to HQ and that's all there is to it." Nixon crossed his arms over his chest, attempting to appear imposing from his perch on the edge of the dingy motel bed.

I slammed my hand against the doorframe. "We have to continue with the list! It's obvious that someone doesn't want us to get answers, which means—"

"Which means they're going to go a long way to keep us from getting them," Nixon interjected.

"No, it means we need to find those answers because they're important."

"I'm not risking your sanity for those answers." Nixon's eyes flashed with something akin to fear as his jaw clenched.

I choked back a laugh. The man who tinkered with my memories and nearly drove me insane because of it was worried about my mind now? *Un-fucking-believable.* "I'm not going insane, Nixon. I'm addicted to feeling death, completely different."

He snorted. "Yeah, you saying that so nonchalantly totally makes me feel better about the entire situation."

"It's important to get answers." Plus, I needed the time to figure out how to prove Austin's innocence.

"Not as important as everything else right now." Nixon stood and began shoving the small bundle of our blood-encrusted clothing into a plastic bag.

We'd have to take them with us and dispose of them later. Luckily, we'd both had a change of clothes with us, although mine was another cheap outfit I'd gotten courtesy of my elderly helpers. *I wonder what they think happened to me. I wish I could have told them goodbye and thanks.*

Fidgeting, I tried to come up with a last-ditch plan. If Nixon took me back with him before I could track down any information on Natalie's disappearance, then Austin was as good as dead. *Everything that's been happening lately is connected. I know it. But how do I convince Nixon?*

Wait. I could ... no, I can't. But it's the only thing I have to leverage. It's the only thing Nixon truly wants from me. But I can't. I just can't. Austin would never forgive me. Or maybe he would. He wouldn't like it but if it was the only way to save his life ...

Before I lost my nerve, I quickly stripped off all my

clothes while Nixon's back was turned. As he turned his head in my direction, he sucked in a sharp breath and froze.

"What the fuck are you doing?"

Holding his gaze, I sashayed over to him. "What does it look like I'm doing?" Biting my lower lip, I ran my hands down my body.

His pupils dilated and his Adam's apple danced in his throat, but he made no move to touch me. "What the *fuck*, Sam? You think you can use sex to get your way?"

Pressing my body against his, I wrapped my arms around his neck and pursed my lips in silent invitation. When he still didn't respond, I rose onto my tiptoes and brushed my mouth softly against his. His body was vibrating with the need to move, to touch me, but he had become as stiff as a living statue.

But I was not to be deterred. He'd give in eventually. "Fuck me, Nixon. I know it's what you want."

He snatched my wrists, breaking my hold on him forcefully, and swung me around to pin my arms behind my back. His voice was low and gruff when he spoke, his hot breath fanning along my right shoulder. "What's happening right now? Is it a side effect of the death or …"

His grip tightened on me, his breath growing ragged. "Or are you willing to whore yourself out for him? Huh? You think I'll give you what you want for sex? Tell me, Sam," he yanked me against his chest, leaning in to whisper in my ear, "what if I said it would save his life if you left him for me? What would you do then?"

I lurched forward in an attempt to free myself, but he only pressed into me more firmly.

"How far are you willing to go for him?" He nipped at my earlobe.

"Get your fucking hands off of me," I grated.

"You want me to let you go now? I thought you were willing to fuck me? Have you changed your mind already? And what about my proposition? Choose me over him, and I'll make sure he lives."

Turning my head, I snarled, "You don't mean any of it, you're just trying to push my buttons. And congrats, it worked. Now let me go so I can get dressed."

"Answer me this then, would you have gone through with it if I said I'd let Austin go? Would you really have whored yourself out? For him?"

My nostrils flared. "How far would you go to save me? How far would anyone go to save the life of the person that owns their entire soul?"

Nixon flung me away from him. "You disgust me."

Stumbling forward, I snagged my clothes, then pulled them on with jerky movements. "Good. Then maybe you'll realize that loving me always was and will be a mistake for you, and you'll let Austin go because it's the right thing to do."

Nixon's lips pulled back from his teeth in a snarl. "There's evidence of his guilt."

"Yeah, I don't buy it. You don't really believe he had anything to do with the blast. You're just trying to get me away from him again … to save me. But as you saw earlier,

Nixon, without him I'm a lost cause. With him, I stand a chance, even if it is a small one."

"You believe that, don't you? That he might be able to help you?"

"Yes, I do. I really do. He understands what I'm going through, and he has abilities that no one else does. Plus, he loves me. Whether you believe it or not, he does. And, Nixon …"

I waited for his gaze to find mine. "You know after what you saw at that house in Turtle Creek that you definitely can't help me, not now anyways. Maybe before you could have, but now it's too late."

Resignation washed over his features, dulling his eyes. He nodded reluctantly. "All right. I'll see what I can do. But so help me God, if he makes things worse for you, I'll put a bullet right between his eyes and I don't care if you hate me forever. I want you safe more than I want anything else."

Hope exploded in my chest, and I grinned. "I know it won't be easy for you, but I want you to know—"

The motel door burst open, smoke pouring in to fill the air. Nixon slammed into me, taking me to the ground where he covered me protectively. "Stay down. I can't see a thing," he hissed in my ear.

A canister rolled into the room, more smoke trailing in its wake to billow out around us.

"Drop your damn void shield so I can try to figure out what's going on." I coughed, my lungs burning.

As soon as I felt his shield drop, I pushed past Nixon's

emotions to reach out in all directions. Gasping, my lungs on fire, I tried to focus, fighting as my mind dimmed around the edges.

"Sam," Nixon croaked. "We need to—"

I slipped into unconsciousness with the weight of Nixon crushing into me.

SNAPPING to awareness with my body on high alert, adrenaline coursed through my system, my heart pounding in my ears. I struggled to remain still and silent so that I could ascertain my situation without alerting my captors. Doing a quick mental inventory, I found myself to be sore, but all my appendages were in working order, and I had no intense pain. The worst of my predicament seemed to be a scratchy throat coupled with cottonmouth—both annoying, but nothing to be concerned about.

I couldn't make out any clear sounds to indicate that I was alone, so I slitted my eyes to peek out from behind my lashes. I was lying on a cot, unbound, in a room that could pass for a prison cell besides the fact that there were no bars.

The handle on the door turned, and I closed my eyes to feign still being knocked out. Two masculine voices could be heard having a whispered conversation as the door creaked open slowly.

"Shouldn't she be awake by now?"

"Don't worry, all of her vitals are fine. I wouldn't be worried just yet."

"Yeah, well, you'd be concerned, too, if your life was on the line. You're just the hired help."

"After seeing what we're dealing with, don't kid yourself into thinking if we fuck this up I won't lose my life, too. I'd be a loose end. If I'd known, I never would have taken this job. But I'm thinking we should have killed the guy she was with. I'm also thinking—"

"That's a lot of thinking, and no one is paying you to think. The guy she was with, Nixon, I was ordered to not harm him. You kill him, you die."

"Good to—" The door clicked shut, muffling the rest of the conversation.

Shit. I hadn't learned much, but I was relieved to know Nixon was alive and unharmed. Although it was puzzling as to who would have me abducted and also care about his well-being. Beyond that, I had to wonder why I was abducted this time. As pathetic as it was, the whole process was beginning to become old hat to me. At least my captors wanted me alive. And something about that little tidbit had me more convinced than ever that Natalie's disappearance, the list, the murders … everything was connected.

A wave of nausea crashed into me, and I curled into myself, saliva pooling in my mouth. Hopefully, the aftereffects of whatever was in the smoke bombs wouldn't last much longer. My thoughts of course went to Austin, and I reached out to him mentally.

"Austin, I need you."

"Chl— Sam," Austin's voice immediately responded in my mind.

The fact that he started to call me Chloe, my birth name, worried me. He hardly ever slipped. In fact, I couldn't recall the last time he did.

"Austin, what's wrong? Tell me what's happening with you."

"I'm fine, I don't matter right now. Where are you? Are you hurt? Talk to me."

"I'm fine, a little sick from the chemical assault, but they don't seem to want to harm me, and Nixon is—"

"Here, with me. We're trying to track you, but something's wrong. We can't seem to— Do you know what they want?"

Nixon freed Austin to help track me down. Which meant Austin was safe, for now. Relief wound its way through me, easing a bit of my tension. *"I don't know what they want. They don't know I'm awake yet. I—"*

The door slammed open, and I jolted upright, doing my best to prepare myself for whatever would happen next, but nothing could have prepared me for what did.

A young, white girl was unceremoniously tossed into the room by an unseen person, the door quickly closing behind her. I rushed forward, my knees thumping on the concrete as I dropped down beside her. Brushing her matted blonde hair out of her ashen face, I noted her shallow breathing and the way her eyes darted back and forth behind closed lids. There were no obvious signs of injury, but I sensed the dark shadow of death looming regardless.

Trembling, I rocked back on my heels, gaze riveted to her prone form, wanting to resist, but knowing my efforts would be futile.

Giving in, I slipped into her mind.

This can't be happening to me. I'm only six months away from my twenty-first birthday. I'm so cold … can't breathe … I'm dying and I'm thinking about my twenty-first birthday. Maybe I am as vapid as Jason said I am. Jason … I'll never see him again … never get a chance to prove him wrong. Why didn't I ever tell him I had feelings for him? Now he'll never know … can't feel my fingers anymore … can't feel … Jason … my family … none of them … I'll never see any of them aga—

I stayed with her until the end, sucking down her sadness along with every last bit of regret. The flavor of her death was just right—the combination of her youth and the suddenness of it—my favorite kind. Yes, she would die, and I would go on. She would—.

My concentration abruptly shifted as I made the horrifying realization that Austin had remained connected to me while I was feeling the girl's death. His euphoria wrapped itself around mine, the extent of it letting me know that he truly didn't have to be physically close by. All he needed was for me to be linked with him … and together we could experience the highs of death.

Oh God. Revulsion twisted my stomach and I lurched over, digging my nails into the concrete, saliva dribbling off my chin as I dry heaved. *What am I doing to him?* I was tainting Austin just like I feared I would. Weighing him down instead of letting him pull me up. Throwing up a haphazard mental shield, I slammed the door shut on him and the girl's emotions.

Regrets of my own replaced the *dying*—I glanced at her still form—*make that the* dead *girl's*. I could no longer deny how vast the darkness in me had grown. Nor could I pretend that there was any hope of me being saved.

It was too late for me, but not for Austin. I wouldn't add him to my long list of mistakes. Because I'd made a lot of mistakes in my life. From the way I'd handled things with Nixon and Austin, to how I—

Nope. There were too many fuckups to list, and I couldn't change my past. Going forward, though, I refused to let Austin suffer because of me ever again. I would save him, no matter the cost. And one day he would understand. *Maybe.*

Slumping onto the cot, I pulled my knees up to my chest. I wasn't the self-sacrificing type though. I loved Austin and therefore I didn't want to push him away. The mere thought of losing him again roiled my gut, causing me to question whether I was strong enough to go through with it.

But … Perhaps, I could use Austin's love to motivate me to resist feeling death anymore. I obviously couldn't do it for myself, but for him … for him, I had to try. *No. I'll do more than try. I'll do it. For Austin. I can do anything for him. First, I'll free myself from my captors, whoever the hell they are, and then I'll free myself from my addiction.*

Failure is not an option.

Chapter 16

My arms and legs tingled from holding myself too still for what seemed like an eternity, but I forced myself to remain inert, my legs crossed beneath me on the small cot. Sweat dribbled down my temples and gathered along my upper lip, my breathing shallow, and heart thrashing against my ribcage, belying my outward calm. I didn't want to look, didn't want to acknowledge the heap on the floor that used to be a person but was now nothing more than a shell … and yet my gaze kept finding its way back to the dead girl.

Her long, blonde hair was tangled around her face, mostly obscuring her features, although I could tell she was pretty, maybe even beautiful before death had leached that indefinable quality from her. Obviously, she'd been put in the room with me so I could feel her dying emotions … but why? Malcolm was dead and he was the only one who came to mind who might want to push me further down that dark road.

Finally, the door to my prison opened slowly, whining its protest, as two men wearing ski masks stepped in, one black and one red. The second one across the threshold, Mr. Black Mask, closed the door behind him. I resisted the urge to slip into their minds to garner their emotions, because in order for that to happen I would have to drop my mental shield, and that wasn't something I was ready to do at the moment. Besides, I wasn't sure what offensive skills they might have. For all I knew there was a bevy of gifted people at my unknown captor's disposal to help them complete their task, whatever that was.

I smirked at the masked man standing closer to me, Mr. Red Mask. "Really? You're afraid of me seeing your faces?"

Ignoring my comment, Mr. Red Mask spoke. "We're not going to hurt you. We—"

I snorted. "You already have, dimwit. You think I *want* to feel people's death emotions?"

He tilted his head in silent challenge.

"Fine, so I enjoy feeling them, but I don't want to enjoy feeling them. It's kind of like I'm a drug addict. So please be so kind as to *not* offer me the drugs."

"We need you to take the drugs," Mr. Black Mask said flatly.

I narrowed my eyes at him. "Why?"

"Can't tell you that," Mr. Red Mask said quickly. "Just know that if you cooperate, then we'll let you go sooner."

I didn't like where the conversation seemed to be heading. "And what exactly do I need to do to cooperate?"

"Enjoy the deaths we provide for you."

Shock, anticipation, anger, and a myriad of other emotions rolled through me in quick succession. "Why? Why are you doing this to me?" My voice held an edge of desperation I wished I could hide. It wasn't going to do me any good to show any weakness in my current situation.

"Look," Mr. Red Mask started, "I don't want to be doing this to you. I can't imagine what it must be like, but I have no choice."

I stood abruptly, causing both men to back away from me. "You don't have to do this. Tell me who's forcing your hands and we can help you track them, kill them if need be. Just please, please don't do this to me. I don't want to become—" My voice cracked, and I swallowed the rest, internally chastising myself for begging.

Mr. Red Mask bowed his head, and for a moment I thought maybe I'd gotten through to him, causing hope to bloom in my chest. But he kept his gaze averted as he responded, "I'm sorry. Really I am. Just please cooperate so this will all be over as quickly as possible ... for all of us."

Anger surged, bubbling like hot lava in my center. My shields began to slip as the hostile emotions built, swirling through me, and forming into a weapon. The dark energy snapped from my body and hurtled headlong into Mr. Red Mask, causing him to drop to the ground like a bag of stones. He cried out in pain, and I turned my focus on Mr. Black Mask, smiling. He took several hesitant steps back, seemingly sizing me up in order to decide how best to engage me. Luckily for me, he didn't know that I wasn't strong enough to do that kind of mental attack again so soon, and that I would need some recovery time. It was quite possible I wouldn't need to though, and that I could bluff him into submission.

"Let me go and I won't hurt you," I snarled.

With my full attention on Mr. Black Mask, I didn't notice that Mr. Red Mask was back in play, and without any kind of warning a dart sank into my thigh. I let out a startled grunt as my leg went instantly numb, causing me to stagger.

Tugging the small bit of metal and plastic from my leg, my wavering gaze locked onto it with disbelief. "I can't believe I got tranqued again."

First Nixon, and now these people.

Both men clambered for the door, making a hasty retreat before I could react.

The dart fell from my fingers and clattered to the floor as I stumbled back to the cot, my head swimming, and my gut roiling. "Just for the record," I slurred, collapsing on my side, "I'm over this whole losing consciousness against my will thing." I swallowed, my tongue thick in my mouth. "Plus, who the fuck knows what kind of interactions the different drugs in my system might do? You better hope the mixture doesn't kill me."

My gaze found its way to the dead girl yet again. "And

for fuck's sake, get this body out of here before it starts to reek."

I waited for the drugs to force me into oblivion, but miraculously I managed to stay conscious, even though all I seemed to have control over was my eyelids, which I blinked slowly.

Mr. Black Mask entered the room, leaving a moment later with the girl's stiff body in tow. Another few minutes ticked by before Mr. Red Mask moved into my field of vision, approaching me slowly. He sank down on his haunches so I had full view of his masked face and light-colored eyes.

"I didn't know you could do that, hurt people with your mind. You really are as strong as they said, and I'm—I'm truly sorry for what we're doing, but you have to understand that I don't have a choice."

He dipped his head, breaking eye contact. "I don't want to become like you and the rest of them. If I give them what they want—you—then I have a chance. They promised." A fine tremor ran over his body. "I don't want to be like all of you." His voice cracked and he stood. "It's too late for you, but not for me." He shuffled slowly to the door, pausing to look at me over his shoulder once more before leaving.

As per usual, my thoughts immediately turned to Austin. I yearned to share with him the bits and pieces of information that I'd learned, to discuss theories—fuck, just hear his voice. But I couldn't let him enjoy death with me again. I had to save him. I had to be stronger for him.

If I was as skilled as Austin, then I could keep any death emotions separate—compartmentalize them. But I lacked the ability to close off parts of my mind, and because of it, I would have to temporarily sacrifice my connection to the man I loved to protect him. I refused to allow Austin to become as addicted as Malcolm, as me, and as it seemed all empaths who came into contact with death seemed to become.

Is that what Mr. Red Mask meant by not wanting to become like the rest of us? Was he an empath, too? Would I find his name on the list that Nixon had pilfered from the first empath's house? How were we all connected? The unanswered questions were stacking up and threatening to drive me insane.

But no matter, as soon as the drugs that were keeping me temporarily immobilized wore off, I'd execute a brilliant escape plan and then I'd track down the answers I so desperately needed. I internally smiled. *Even if I have to make a few people bleed in the process. And the best part is I won't even need to worry about feeling guilty for enjoying those types of deaths.*

Chapter 17

Time crept by slow as molasses as I waited for something to happen … anything really. The return of masked Tweedle Dee and Tweedle Dum, another dying person to be hurled into my prison, or at the very least for my bodily needs to be attended to such as food, water, or hell, even the ability to use the toilet. But a big fat nope to any of those options, which definitely didn't do my seething rage any favors.

Clearly, it was another facet of their plan to break me, which in turn had me contemplating a full shutdown of my emotions. It would essentially be a Band-Aid slapped over my gaping problem, but it would solve my desire to feel death for the time being. Of course, I could only remain closed off for so long before risking a meltdown when I turned them back on, basically exasperating my issues.

The rage coursing through my body and burning

through my veins was the only thing keeping me going, exhaustion—both physical and mental—temporarily taking the back seat. As I paced the small room, I rolled through images of sinking my fists into the flesh and bone of my faceless enemies on repeat, the level of hostility riding my system like nothing I'd ever experienced before.

I'm not going to be forced into situations where I'm made to do things I don't want to do anymore. I'm done being the victim. So fucking done. I will take back control of my own damn life and anyone who tries to stand in my way is going to pay.

A dark, familiar laugh echoed softly through the room, and my heart took off at a gallop. Whirling, I staggered back when my gaze met Malcolm's doe-like, brown eyes. He leaned casually against the door, his arms and legs crossed, as a smirk slowly curled his lips upward.

I was rushing towards him before I made a conscious decision to move, my fingers itching to sink into his throat, my fists craving the—

He disappeared right before my eyes, and I slammed awkwardly into the door, the impact jarring. "What the fuck?" I growled. "Am I now completely insane or is he a gho—"

Malcolm's answer came from behind me. "I'm not a ghost, and as far as you being completely insane … well, even if I wasn't a figment of your imagination, I wouldn't exactly be a good judge of that, would I?"

Turning slowly, I let my eyes travel the length of him from his disheveled brown hair down to his slightly worn sneakers. He seemed so real. Every little detail just as I remembered. I shook my head, hoping to dislodge his image somehow. "Fuck. I have completely lost it."

Malcolm, or the perfect facsimile of him, laughed again. "Or maybe I'm just a manifestation of a part of you that you don't want to claim as your own? Ever see *Fight Club*?"

I snorted. "So what, you're like my Tyler Durden now?"

"Hardly," he retorted as he began to pace. "I think I was conjured up by your mind to help get you out of here. Ironic, don't you think? You know, because the treatment they have planned for you is exactly what I tried to do to you myself."

"Yeah, yeah, yeah." I waved him on impatiently. "Apparently this version of you is just as annoying as the real Malcolm was. How about getting to the point instead of rambling," I narrowed my eyes. "on and on. And on."

"All right then." He graced me with a dazzling and no less creepy smile. "Follow me." He marched over to the door and tugged it open.

At least this Malcolm is a lot more agreeable.

It was then I registered what he'd done, and I stared at the open door in confusion. "But how … what … I don't understand. You're not real."

He shrugged, stepping through the door into the hallway. "Real enough." When I didn't immediately follow, he glanced over his shoulder. "Coming?"

But I couldn't seem to make myself move. I was immobilized by uncertainty. *I'm insane. I've lost my fucking mind.* There was no other explanation. Malcolm appearing to me a la *Fight Club* style was the big, blinking sign announcing my complete breakdown. There was no way that door was actually open unless …

If Malcolm was appearing as a part of me like Tyler Durden, then everything Malcolm did was really me. Which meant that I was the one who somehow just opened the door. When I looked at it that way, it made sense … sort of. Deciding I had nothing left to lose, especially my mind, I scurried after him.

"How do you know where you're going?" I demanded when I caught up to him.

He rolled his eyes. "Because you do."

I shook my head emphatically. "But I don't. I was unconscious when they brought me here."

"Well, then it beats me because I only know what you know, and I happen to know exactly where I'm going." He continued to stride with self-confidence down the hallway.

I trailed along after him, my eyes darting around the office-like building warily. At any moment someone could pop out to prevent our—

My escape. It can't be this easy, it just can't be.

Vertigo slammed into me, my world tilting as I dipped my head to see blood running down my hands. Staggering, I reached out to support myself on the nearest wall, my gaze transfixed on the crimson smears I left on the white paint.

Malcolm cackled, turning towards me with glee

plastered across his face. He held a man in front of him, one arm banded around his chest, and the other poised with a knife at his throat. "Well, go ahead, I know you want to." He dragged the blade across the man's throat, throwing his head back to cackle again.

The man's body crumpled to the floor, and between one blink and the next, it was me standing over it, not Malcolm. Disgust, revulsion ... and excitement swirled in my gut as my adrenaline spiked.

No, stop. Don't do it. You can't. But ... but he's dying anyways now. There's really no point in wasting it. You can get your fix and make it your last time. Yes, one last trip into death before giving it up completely.

A delighted shiver ran up my spine as I slipped into his mind.

He was choking on his own blood, the warm liquid bubbling into his throat and mouth. I inhaled, tasting and smelling the coppery tang at the same time. He—I gurgled. It was in that last moment that he—I knew it had all been a setup. They were never going to let Cal go, and the second he hired me my death had been sealed, too. Nothing was as it seemed. But after all the shady things I'd done in my life, I had a feeling I'd die violently one day, I just hadn't thought today was that day.

I inhaled deeply as his heart beat one last time, hesitating forever.

He's dead. He's dead and I killed him. Not Malcolm, but me. The enormity of the situation settled in my chest, cinching my heart.

But there, lingering in my mind, like a string left

behind, I sensed the person behind my little hallucinations. As it turned out, Mr. Red Mask, aka Cal, was more than a weak empath. He'd slipped right past my mental shields to manipulate my brain into seeing Malcolm. And it went beyond just that. I'd been essentially forced to murder someone in cold blood so that I could enjoy that death. I was officially one step closer to being like Malcolm and Maggie, or was I one step closer to being like Maggie and Austin like Malcolm?

No. No. I can't let that happen. I won't let us become like them.

Dropping to my knees, I pounded on the ground, choking back a sob as fresh anger burned through me. "Why? Why do you want us to be this way? What purpose does it serve?"

Austin. Shit. What about Austin? Since my mental shield was breached, did that mean he enjoyed the latest death right along with me? Had I failed him again so soon? Tentatively I reached out to him, getting nothing. Maybe I'd gotten lucky for once and Nixon had managed to shield him.

Pulling myself to my feet, I shoved aside all unnecessary emotions, steeling myself for what I had to do next. Tugging on the mental link, I focused on Cal. "I'm coming for you."

Now that I knew what he was capable of, Cal no longer had the edge. I could taste the acidic flavor of his fear, sensing how close he was. I smirked to myself. "Poor Cal. I guess they didn't tell you all about me after all."

Whoever 'they' were. Well, I was about to find out.

Cal wasn't sequestered away in some well-guarded room like I expected. In fact, it turned out he was merely a few doors down from me all by his lonesome. It was almost too easy, as if I was meant to find him. And with the way things were going, I probably was, all of it just another part of the game. Although I couldn't bring myself to care at the moment.

I wiggled my fingers in greeting as I stalked towards him. "Well, hello there."

Cal was sitting in a computer chair at a small desk, his ski mask perched on top of his head like a hat, his thin face exposed to me. As I neared him, his hazel eyes widened with shock and dawning horror.

Scrambling back, he raised his thin, pale arms into the air, cowering against the wall. "Please, I didn't have a choice."

But he wasn't as frail and timid as he wanted me to believe. Without any mental shields to speak of since he had left himself wide open to slip into my mind, I was able to read exactly what he was doing. And he was attempting to play me for a fool again, by plucking any note of sympathy he could manage.

I bared my teeth in a snarl. "If you don't want me to kill you, then you better start talking."

"I-I—" he started, his voice still trembling with supposed fear.

"Oh come off it," I growled. "You're trying to feel my emotions to figure out how to play on my sympathies. So tell me, is it working?" I shoved my simmering rage at him.

Dropping his arms, Cal sat up, meeting my gaze levelly. "It was worth a shot." He shrugged, a lopsided smirk curling one side of his mouth up. "If you don't kill me, then I'll tell you everything I know, but first I want you to promise to help me. I really am a victim. I just might have been playing up my vulnerability for your sake a bit."

I quirked my eyebrow. "A bit?"

He shifted in his seat, his smirk growing into a grin. "Okay, a lot. But everything I told you was true. The tone in which I delivered the information made no difference."

I tapped my foot in a steady rhythm on the floor. "Yeah, and why shouldn't I just kill you and siphon all the same info from your mind as you die? Seems a lot simpler to me, and a lot less hassle."

"Because you don't really want to kill me?" he asked hesitantly.

Glancing down at the dried blood on my hands, I grimaced. "I'm not so sure I care about such things anymore. After all, I don't know you. Besides myself, the only person I care about is Austin."

"Even with all of your … talents, I don't think you can keep me alive longer than what's natural to die, unless you're suddenly into torture now? I know too much for you to get in the short amount of time it would take me to die otherwise."

Could I torture someone for information? It certainly

would yield a glorious high when I finally let him die. The tentacles of darkness writhed inside of me, screaming out for it—needing it. I shuddered, goose bumps erupting along my arms.

No. I have to resist. For Austin. "I won't torture you. Although I'm sure you can feel how much I want to now that you brought up the idea."

Cal's face molded into genuine fear, and he gulped convulsively. "Yeah, I feel it."

"All right, then we understand each other." Crossing my arms over my chest, I leaned against the wall, staring at him expectantly. "So start spilling."

"Wh-Where should I start?"

"Where every good story starts, Cal, at the beginning."

A little while later Cal had shared everything he knew. It was less than I was hoping for, but more information than I started with, so at least I was heading in the right direction. He knew about the list of names, and that everyone on said list possessed a unique ability. But he didn't know who made the list or what it meant.

He confirmed that I was being targeted with the goal of pushing me over the edge in my internal struggle with death emotions. The big questions were left unanswered though. Such as the two empaths who were serial killers … had they been targeted as well, or were they just a means to an end to get to me? Perhaps we were all part of some twisted study, or quite possibly someone wanted something specific that none of us had given them yet and they would keep searching until some empath delivered it to them.

Cal also told me that he had been approached and threatened by a man who claimed that if he helped flip me, then Cal would be free to go. Not only that, but the man had promised to give him the secret of how to prevent himself from becoming like the rest of us … addicted to death emotions.

I reluctantly agreed to take Cal with me to HQ and to do my best to help him. The thing was, I didn't believe what he'd told me. Maybe he thought he was telling the truth, but I knew better. Austin and I had been set up, only to have me taken hostage after I stumbled upon two empaths who were killed before I could get any real information from them … and then I suddenly find myself in the position to escape with Cal? There was no way it was going to be that simple. Whoever was pulling the strings in the operation seemed ten steps ahead of me up until now, so …. what, they all go out for a cigarette break at the same time? I wasn't buying any of it.

I was currently a pawn in an unknown game, but I'd been positioned perfectly. For it was obvious that there were layers upon layers of lies that I needed to peel away when it came to everyone and everything … except Austin. He was the only person I knew I could trust for sure, even if he was trapped in the same game.

I just hoped that once the truth was finally revealed it didn't turn out to be more horrifying than the lies I'd been living with.

Chapter 18

After everything that happened, it felt surreal to simply hop on an airplane and head to Virginia, but that's exactly what Cal and I did—board a commercial flight like any normal person, as if we weren't both steeped in blood from playing an unknown game with unknown players.

I was edgy and paranoid, my nerves worn and frayed. The people around me seemed to float by in happy bubbles of ignorance, which only heightened the level of surrealness. Hopefully, they would never know how lucky they were to not know the kind of horrors the world held, unlike me who couldn't seem to escape them despite my best efforts.

But beyond anything, as always, I craved Austin. To simply lie in his arms and to hear his heartbeat under my ear. It was the mundane things that pushed to the forefront of my mind. The way he could never seem to put his dirty clothes in the hamper, or how he had the tendency to sleep diagonally across the bed. I even longed for a dose of his abnormally-sized ego. The good, the bad —it made him who he was … the man I fell in love with despite my desire not to. And I missed everything about him.

My mind slipped back to the first time we'd ever had sex when I'd been dating Nixon, and he'd been fucking Jessica.

His nostrils flared, the only warning that his control had snapped. He shoved me against the wall, his hand gripping my throat tightly, as his lips seared mine. I grunted in dismay even as I met his desperate tongue with matched fervor.

His hand flexed against my throat as he ground against me, my leg already hooked around his waist. His touch burned and soothed, excited, and calmed my inner turmoil because maybe us being together was a betrayal and a mistake, but it was my betrayal and my mistake, all of what I was doing my choice with no outside emotions cluttering my mind. And I wanted this —him like I never wanted anyone or anything before.

"I need you, Chloe." Austin's heated breath skated over my flesh as he kissed his way down my neck.

"Yes," I moaned, throwing my head back to allow him better access. "I need you, too."

"We need to go somewhere." He'd somehow managed to get my shirt up, capturing my nipple between his teeth. "Can't do this here."

"Your room," I rasped.

"No … Jessica," he said around my other nipple.

Irrational anger caused my gut to clench. Then I remembered Nixon. He was waiting for me in my room. Guilt replaced every other emotion.

I pushed at Austin's chest. "No, Austin, we can't. What about Nixon? He's your best friend."

Austin's voice was low and gruff with unspoken promises of pleasure. "I need you."

He offered me no other explanation, no argument, no rationalizations, just that he needed to be with me, plain and simple. And I wanted it—oh how I wanted it. I wanted him in any and every way he would let me have him.

What little will I had to resist melted away as he stumbled, with me wrapped around his waist, into a nearby room. He yanked my shirt off and deposited me on a desk. Leaning back, I clutched the edge of the scarred wood as Austin tugged my pants and underwear off. The cool air skated over my overheated flesh, causing goose bumps to erupt.

Austin paused, his gaze running over me from head to toe, as if he was planning what to do with me next. I swallowed, my throat suddenly as dry as the Sahara.

"You're so beautiful," he said, echoing Nixon's words the first time we'd been together.

I forced my mind away from the guilt that knowledge brought with it.

He shucked his clothes quickly, coming to stand between my quivering thighs. It was my turn to give his naked body the once over. He was exactly how I'd imagined him—perfect. I knew it was ridiculous to even think, but to me he was. Austin was absolutely perfect in that moment. His long, lean muscles gleamed with a fine sheen of sweat, his toned abs flexing under my scrutiny as I drew my gaze down the line of his body ... lower, lower, and lower until it snagged on his massive erection.

I gulped. I knew he was large, I'd felt him before, but seeing him standing there in front of me, completely naked and ready to go ... it was both intimidating and awe-inspiring.

I abruptly hooked my legs around his back, causing him to pitch forward. Grabbing his hair, I pulled him down until he was mere inches from my face, our breath intermingling. My lips curled up at the corners as I said, "Fuck me, Austin. Fuck me now."

His eyes flashed as a pained sound erupted from the back of his throat, his nostrils flaring. I threw my head back when he plunged into me. His fingers bit into my hips as he pulled out and slammed back in, falling into a brutal, demanding rhythm. The desk inched its way across the floor, the metal legs scraping loudly, blending with our moans and grunts. Oh, yes. Yes, this is what I want—need. *I'd never had rough sex before, but then again, I'd never been running on my own emotions during sex before either.*

Austin gripped the sides of my face, forcing my head down. "Look at me, Chloe," he growled. "I want you to look at me when you come."

As if his words gave me the permission I needed, my body exploded in pleasure, and I screamed. Austin held me steady even as I tried to thrash my head, his gaze capturing mine for the entirety of my unraveling, followed shortly after by his. His eyes held a single-minded intensity that spoke of possession, and passion, and in that moment, we completely belonged to each other—and each other alone.

A silence fell over us, even as our hearts thrummed in our chests like hummingbirds. I kept my breathing shallow, afraid if I moved, I'd break the trance, this one perfect moment when nothing else mattered but us.

Austin moved first, gliding his thumb over my bottom lip. I nipped at him playfully, which caused him to dip his head to deliver me a long, sensual kiss, much different from the ones he'd given me minutes earlier.

Threading my fingers into his hair, I pulled, eliciting a grunt of approval from him. As our kiss deepened, I felt him grow hard inside of me again. I rocked my hips in encouragement. The slow, steady rhythm he built was the opposite of what we'd just done, but I realized they were both things I craved from Austin. I want him in any and every way he'll let me have him.

Squeezing my eyes shut, my muscles coiled and then spasmed, my heart pounding out of my chest. But Austin didn't stop, not yet, and my pleasure continued with each deliberate thrust. I clawed at his back, arching up when he finally spilled his release, pumping slowly, as I clenched around him. I never wanted it to stop. Me. Him. Us. I needed him to be with me forever.

I'd still been Chloe, the most naïve version of myself, and someone I would never be again. I'd given my body fully to Austin before admitting that he already owned my heart. Something that, if I was being honest with myself, he'd owned from the beginning. The only thing that made the whole situation bearable was the fact that I owned his heart, too. We belonged to each other completely, and although our love had hurt those around us, that same love gave us strength. Austin and I were selfish and flawed, only really caring about each other. Because, in the end, the people we hurt didn't matter, only we did.

Which made our love toxic. I couldn't deny it any longer. But unlike before when we'd merely emotionally hurt those close to us, the potential fallout from our relationship could be catastrophic enough to end lives. Even knowing that terrifying fact, I wasn't sure I could do the right thing.

Had I become like Heathcliff, unable to let go no matter who I destroyed by my actions? I kept coming back to that question over and over, and yet when I walked into the airport terminal and saw Austin waiting for me, his beautiful face lighting up the instant our gazes met, I knew with one hundred percent certainty what my answer would always be … I could never willingly walk away from him. Never. All consequences be damned.

Moving as quickly as I could without breaking into a sprint, everything but Austin blurred into the background. I needed to touch him, to feel his skin under my fingertips. I needed to lose myself in him completely. With a squeal, I flung myself into his waiting arms.

"My good Sammy girl," he murmured just before slanting his lips over mine.

I opened up to him both physically and mentally, wanting

to share every part of myself with him. I swore I wouldn't do it, and I knew it was wrong to let him feel the deaths since the cravings had begun in him, but I needed him completely in that moment—his understanding, his love, his body.

Ultimately, I was too selfish to deny myself connecting with him on any level. That was one of the many problems of being an empath—we always went with our emotions first, our base instincts winning out over common sense in any given situation. I knew what I should do, but instead in my desperation to feel as close to Austin as possible, I let him into my mind completely, dropping all barriers.

Temporarily forgetting where we were, I wrapped my legs around his waist, grinding my already dripping center against him. He knew what I needed, and he craved it just as much as I did. His grip on my ass tightened as he groaned into my mouth.

"For fuck's sake," Nixon growled.

"I guess that's Austin," Cal said.

"I'll take care of it," Taryn said, then, "Austin. Austin, come on man, we talked about this."

Austin's fingers flexed, and he groaned again, this one pained, before he finally relinquished me, reluctantly breaking our kiss. Snapping out of my mind, he set me on my feet.

In a daze, I reached for Austin, hating the loss of him on both levels. I wanted—no, needed him inside of me. For him to fuck me as hard as he could while his mind touched mine. Sweat dribbled down my spine, my system ready to combust. *Please, I need—*

I shook my head, finally remembering where we were. *You're an adult. Not a teenager. You can wait. You. Can. Wait. You. Can. Wait ...*

Sensing my internal battle, Austin scooped me up in his arms, cradling me to his chest. His muscles trembled with the effort to keep things PG-13 as he started to move through the terminal with me clinging to him, my face buried in the crook of his neck. The strong rhythm of his heart soothed me. The morbid thought that if it ever stopped beating, mine would too, slithered through my mind. *I could never live without him.*

When we got to our transportation—another SUV—Austin clambered inside with me still in his arms. Realizing we were technically no longer in public, I began pushing at his mental shields, desiring a complete connection with him again. While still attempting to break past his barriers, I lifted my face to nibble on his earlobe. He groaned, his erection pushing at my ass as I settled onto his lap. Gliding my hands into his hair, I tugged gently and wriggled against him, causing another groan, a louder one to erupt from the back of his throat.

"Have a little sympathy. Ten minutes, just give me ten minutes alone with my wife," Austin rumbled to our unwanted company.

Taryn was the one who responded, "I'm sorry, man, you know the deal."

Whipping my head around, I sought out Nixon's gaze.

"Please," I begged, putting more of my plea into my eyes than my voice. "I need him."

It was wrong. I knew it was wrong. Another thing to add to the growing list of things that made me a bad person. Because I should have felt shame or embarrassment at the least, but again ... I was selfish and I knew Nixon loved me. It wasn't my fault that he continued to ignore my warnings about pursuing me. I'd been honest about loving Austin on a level beyond reason. But, since Nixon left me no other options, I would use his misplaced feelings to manipulate him if I could, and he had no one to blame but himself if I hurt him again.

Nixon's voice cracked. "When we get back to HQ you two ... you two can have some time." His eyes left mine as his jaw muscles jumped, and he sucked in a few shallow breaths, as if it physically hurt him to witness me with Austin.

I was being cruel, and yet I couldn't bring myself to truly care anymore. Once, I did. At least I think I did. In what seemed like some far-off time and place I remembered caring about the people I hurt. Now, it seemed like just another false memory or dream.

Somewhere along the line, I'd changed, and I wasn't exactly sure why. I was positive Nixon would blame Austin, and maybe he was right to some degree, but Nixon had also contributed by attempting to steal away my life under the guise of protection. The truth was, there were too many ingredients in the recipe used to form the new callous me.

Although I wasn't the only one who had changed. Nixon was no longer the same easy-going, good-natured man I'd once known. And Austin wasn't the closed-off player he once was. In fact, Austin had become a one-woman man—completely and utterly devoted to me and only me.

My heart fisted in my chest as clarity settled over me. I loved Austin unconditionally. And I trusted him with everything that I was. Which meant I didn't care if he'd been with a thousand women while he thought I was dead. All that mattered was the now, and the now was us, together for as long as we could make that happen.

Leaning in close, I whispered in his ear, "I don't care if you were with anyone or a thousand anyones when you thought I was dead—my feelings for you will never change. Nothing will ever stop me from loving you. What I feel for you is unconditional."

He pulled away just enough so his gaze could sweep over my features, and then peering into my eyes, his baby blues darkening a few shades, he asked, "You mean that?"

I bit my lower lip, smiling at him shyly. "It's us against the world. Isn't it?"

"Yeah, it is." He captured my lips with his again.

I idly registered twin groans of displeasure from both Cal and Taryn who were sitting in front of us, and tense silence from Nixon, but my world narrowed down to only Austin again. There we stayed, pressed up against each other, making out and groping each other with no regard for anyone or anything around us for the entire ride back to HQ.

When we finally arrived at our destination, I resumed my position of pressing my face into Austin's neck so I didn't have to acknowledge anything but him, and he scooped me back into his arms to carry me.

"Hurry," I murmured against his intoxicating skin. Austin's fingers gripped me more firmly, and I was jostled roughly as he did in fact pick up his pace.

When we reached our room in the compound of HQ, Austin kicked our door shut with his booted foot and came crashing down onto the bed with me. For a moment we were all clashing teeth, lips, and skin before Austin pulled back to meet my gaze.

He curled a piece of my newly darkened hair around his finger. "I like it, but I like your natural color better."

I covered his hand with mine. "I didn't think I had a choice, but it was a waste of time."

"I know," he said. "You already showed me everything, and now it's my turn."

He yanked me into his mind, opening up the one place I'd been afraid to see since I'd regained my memories.

Bits and pieces of anguish, bitterness, and depression twisted together and spiraled past me, but then one vivid memory rose up, snatching all of my attention.

Austin sat at a dimly lit bar with Taryn, the latter laughing and flirting with the many women who approached them. But Austin only had eyes for the massive quantity of liquor he was consuming.

After slamming down another shot of amber-colored liquid, he turned to Taryn, his voice slurring slightly. I was betting no one would notice but me though. Austin held his liquor well, or rather he hid his levels of intoxication well. "Let's get out of here. I'm bored."

One of the women talking to Taryn stepped closer to Austin, flashing him a dazzling grin. "I'm sure I can find you something amusing to do."

She was tall, blonde, and leggy. I didn't want to see what happened next, but I'd asked for the truth, and Austin was giving it to me, for better or worse.

Austin tilted his head at her, sneering. "I'm really not looking for a quick fuck in the bathroom, but thanks." He then turned to Taryn again. "I said let's get out of here. I can't take it anymore."

"You're a fucking asshole," the blonde woman hissed at Austin. "I would never get it on with anyone, let alone you, in a public restroom."

Austin flicked his gaze back in her direction. "Tell it to someone who believes you. You're easy, sweetheart, and everyone here knows it. So you can stop pretending to be offended."

Her face flushed and she started to say something, but her friend stepped forward to whisper in Austin's ear. "Taryn told me about your wife." She ran her hand down Austin's arm. "It's okay, baby, I can make you feel better. And I don't even care if you feel the need to insult me."

"That's because you like it," Austin snapped at her. "And I don't—"

She raised her French-manicured hands up to quiet him. "I want to suck your cock, no strings. You can even close your eyes and pretend I'm her, it won't bother me."

"Go ahead," Taryn encouraged. "I know you miss her, I get that, but you're not a monk, and man—it's been over two years now."

Austin grunted, letting himself be led away by the small brunette woman. Once inside the handicapped stall in the Ladies Room, she dropped to her knees in front of Austin and unzipped his pants, liberating his cock. He closed his eyes and slumped back against the wall as she slid him into her mouth. He groaned, fisting her hair.

Jealously burned in my gut despite everything. I'd just learned that for two years Austin had been celibate, and he clearly didn't really want this girl, but it was a little hard to think rationally when I was seeing another woman with her lips wrapped around my husband's cock.

"Sammy ... my good Sammy girl ..." Austin mumbled as he began to control the rhythm the brunette sucked him off with his hands that he had in her hair.

Well, at least I knew he was thinking of me, and as twisted as it was it kind of made me feel better. After all, it wasn't like he had been cheating on me since he thought I was dead.

Austin's head fell back and his body tensed. The brunette made a choking sound as he came in her mouth and forced her all the way down on him to take it. That was something I enjoyed, but I knew some women didn't.

When he was finished, the brunette stood, a pissed-off expression on her face. "What the fuck? I couldn't breathe."

Austin's eyes snapped open, and he seemed to realize through his drunken haze that he hadn't been with me. "Get the fuck out," he growled, tucking himself back into his pants.

The brunette's lips pressed into a thin line, and she spun on her heels to make her exit, but not before leaving him with a parting sentiment. "You're a fucking asshole, Candy's right."

Austin barked out a laugh. "Of course her name is Candy, of course it is."

With that, the brunette left in a huff and Austin turned to the toilet. "Fuck." He leaned over it and dry heaved. "Fuck, Sam, fuck, I'm sorry." He ran his hand through his messy hair and slumped onto the disgusting floor.

The stall door swung open a moment later and Taryn entered. "Shit. Let's get you out of here. I was just trying to help. You know that, right, man?" He leaned down and helped Austin to his feet.

"You're a good friend, Taryn. It's not your fault I'm all fucked up in the head." He chuckled darkly, his head lolling. Taryn supported him with ease as he staggered. "Hell, I was fucked up before Sam, but I didn't know what I was missing. Now I do ... now I do."

More memories, more attempts by Taryn to help him move on, rolled past me in my mind's eye. A lot of it was confusing, garbled, much like Austin had been at the time, but one thing became crystal clear to me. He hadn't been with anyone except the brunette that had blown him. In all the years we'd been separated, him a supposed widower, where he had every right to try and move on ... he hadn't.

It was what I should have wanted. It was what should have made me happy to know, but—

"Oh, God." Tears burned the corners of my eyes and spilled down my cheeks. "You were like that—a complete mess, destroyed—the entire time … and I was happily living as Nixon's wife." I choked back a sob. "I should have known. How did I not know?"

Austin skimmed his lips over the salty trails of my tears. "You eventually figured it out. You—"

"Why didn't you want me to know? Why did you let me think you were with—"

"Because," he pressed gentle kisses along my skin as he began removing my clothes, "until you realized you could love me even if I was with a thousand women, that it didn't change your feelings towards me because I didn't know you were alive—"

Understanding jolted through me. "I would never have accepted that you could love me when I was with Nixon. Now I know it's possible for you to still love me because I would have loved you regardless of how many women you were with."

"Yeah. I didn't want you to feel guilty. Don't, Sam. Don't feel guilty. Please. You're right, now is all that matters. Now and the future, not the time we lost or any of the past. None of that was your fault."

He skimmed his callused hands lovingly over my naked body, dropping to his knees at the foot of the bed as he spread my legs. I shivered when he pressed the side of his face against the inside of my thigh, his warm breath caressing my throbbing clit. As he shifted, the stubble on his face abraded my sensitive flesh, exciting me. I arched up, moaning before his lips touched me.

"I'm still the first man who ever made you come this way and I'll be the last." His words were whispered a hair's breadth away from the tiny bundle of nerves that were crying out for his attention. I resisted the urge to grab Austin's head to force him against me.

He chuckled with satisfaction. "You and I both know Nixon could never do this for you. Your body belongs to me in a way it never could with anyone else, even if you thought you loved him the way you loved me. That love was all for me, never for him. Everything you gave him you were really giving me, and I know that."

He began to lick and suckle me, wrenching noises from my throat that sounded almost inhuman. My legs were pinned down by Austin's hands and dangling helplessly over the bed. I thrashed my head, my body coiling tightly. I was a willing victim of Austin's almost painfully pleasurable assault. When I finally fell over the edge, hurtling towards my orgasm, I screamed his name and clawed mindlessly at his shoulders, seeking some kind of leverage or escape … I wasn't really sure which. He continued his ministrations until I had to push him away because I wanted—*needed* him inside of me.

"Austin, fuck me. Fuck me now."

Sliding fully onto the bed, I opened my arms and legs to him in invitation. His pupils were dilated to the point where only a slim rim of blue showed, making them appear almost black. And those nearly black eyes pinned me in place as he tore his clothes from his body.

"Wait!" I commanded as he touched one knee down on the edge of the comforter. "I just want to look at you for a minute."

I let my eyes roam over every visible inch of him from his dark, messy hair to his toned stomach, to his cock that was glistening with moisture on the tip. "You're perfect," I whispered, not really meaning for him to hear.

His full, succulent lips tipped up at the corners, and his dark, lust-laden eyes twinkled. "I know."

I snorted. "Come here," I commanded, and he obeyed without protest. "Now lie down so I can worship you like you deserve."

"About time," he murmured huskily.

"You should probably shut up before I change my mind. After all, I did already get mine." Despite initially having different intentions, the urge to put him in his place was overwhelming.

"Yeah, but—"

I shut him up by straddling his face. I laughed at the surprise that registered in his eyes, which quickly turned into a moan when he skimmed my clit with his teeth. I grabbed the headboard to steady myself, rocking into Austin as he continued to pleasure me with his mouth. He brought his hands around to knead my ass at the same time. Gazing down at his lust-filled eyes while I rode his face was one of the most erotic things I'd seen to date, and the image alone could have made me come.

My thighs trembled, and I clenched around his tongue, my vision wavering around the edges for a split second. Before I'd even finished spasming, Austin had me flipped over and was plunging into me from behind, my face pressed into the bed with my ass in the air. He gripped a fistful of my hair, tugging roughly. I moaned.

He rode me hard, and I loved every moment of it. When he finally shot his hot release into me, I fell over the edge again, utterly spent. Austin collapsed, pushing me down on the bed while still semi-hard inside of me.

His lips moved against the back of my neck. "It's always so fucking good with you."

I grunted in agreement, falling asleep almost immediately. I was exhausted both physically and emotionally, and I felt safe and satiated in Austin's arms. I just couldn't seem to help myself.

Chapter 19

Leaning over the small hospital bed towards my neighbor, I smiled. "Hi, I'm Chloe, what's your name?" I could feel the boy's worry and trepidation. He didn't like hospitals, and there was something about him that made me want to reassure him.

He blinked his large, luminous eyes and stared back at me. "Hi," he responded shyly. "I'm Kevin."

I plastered my best warm smile on my face, one that I hoped looked like the one my mom gave me often enough. "You know, hospitals aren't that scary, so you shouldn't worry."

He studied me for a moment before saying, "How did you know I'm worried?"

Uh-oh. I slipped up again. *Sometimes I scared people when I knew stuff about their emotions without them telling me. "Lucky guess? So how old are you, Kevin?"*

"Six."

"Me too." I grinned at him. "So, what landed you in here?"

He laughed. "You make it sound like we're in a prison movie or something."

I shrugged. We were both silent a moment, and then he finally answered my question.

"I'm just getting some tests, but you know that probably means I have some kind of cancer."

It was my turn to laugh. "That's just stupid. I'm here for tests, too, and I know I don't have cancer."

He sat up and stared at me with a very serious face. "I'm making a break for it, wanna come with?"

I was always up for some fun. "Sure," I said.

We slipped out of our beds and crept into the dark hallway. There were no nurses or doctors around as far as we could see, so we dashed from doorway to doorway making sort of a game out of it.

"So what are we doing exactly?" I whispered to Kevin.

"We're spying ... going to find out if we're all infected with cancer or maybe something worse."

I scrunched my face up at him. "Worse?"

"Yeah, some kind of flesh-eating bacteria that's gonna make us ooze from the inside out."

"Eeeewww ... I'm not oozing."

"Yet," was all he said before dashing to the next doorway.

But something stopped me short. I felt drawn to explore what was in the room I was in front of. I slid inside silently, making my way to the bed by the window. A beautiful boy laid there, the moonlight from the night spilling across his face. His nearly black hair was sticking up in all directions and he blinked open the bluest eyes I'd ever seen.

"Who are you?" he asked.

I was hit with a feeling of knowing, almost like someone had reached down into me and placed information into my head. "You're going to be very important to me. And I'm going to be just as important to you."

I slapped my hand over my mouth with horror. Why would I say that? It was embarrassing to say such things to a stranger.

He frowned at me. "I know."

"Austin!" I exclaimed, waking with a jolt. Before he had time to react, I shoved the memory I'd just dreamt into his mind.

His eyes widened as he stared down at me blankly, his consciousness turned inward as he watched the scene unfolding in his mind. When it was over, his gaze focused on me. "What the hell was that?"

"So you don't remember any of that either?" I bit the inside of my cheek, watching him carefully.

He frowned. "No, because it didn't happen."

"Then tell me what that was. Kevin the serial killer, I knew him when he was a boy. I showed you how I recognized him when he opened the door, and I had a flash of the memory I just dreamt." I shook my head slowly. "But you're right. I don't remember being in a hospital when I was a kid, and I definitely don't remember meeting you."

His nostrils flared. "Memories can be tampered with. As we all know. But why? And if it really happened, then what does it all mean?"

My mind flashed back to my second encounter with

Austin. At least I thought it was only my second encounter.

"Shhh ... sweetheart. I have you. Everything's going to be fine now."

Warmth and safety wrapped itself around me like a blanket. I allowed my eyes to slide shut as I snuggled into Austin's arms. "You're going to be someone very important to me," I murmured.

"What's she saying now?" Taryn asked.

"Nothing that matters," Austin replied.

Lie. *"Why are you lying to him?" I mumbled, unsure if the words made sense outside of my head.*

"You need to rest. You're confused right now, but when you wake up, you'll be safe, and we'll explain everything."

Annoyance swelled up within me. "Don't patronize me. I'm confused about some things but not that. You're going to be important to me." Exhaustion tugged at my consciousness. "And I'm going to be just as important to you."

"I know." It was the last thing I heard Austin say before everything faded away.

"Austin. It's the same thing I said to you that—"

"Day in the bar. Yeah, I remember. Probably not a coincidence then?"

Scrunching up my face, I said, "I'm thinking no."

"So we knew each other or at least met when we were kids, and you had some kind of premonition about us and what we'd mean to each other."

"Yeah, but so did you. Both times you responded with the same thing."

We fell into silence, both of our minds reeling.

Kevin's name had been on the list Nixon and I found, or at least I remembered seeing *a* Kevin on the list. But I was feeling pretty confident that they were one and the same. If the three of us—Austin, Kevin, and myself—were all on the list, and at the hospital at the same time, did Kevin remember any of it either? Or were his memories tampered with in the same manner that ours seemed to have been? Of course, he was dead, so we'd never find out. Although, again, I was pretty confident that he would be in the same predicament as Austin and me. Why had we been at the hospital at the same time? Was anyone else on the list there as well during that period? And what kind of tests were we given? Did they have something to do with our abilities? I saw no other common thread.

"We need to find out where that list came from," Austin said, breaking me from my inner musings.

"Maybe Cal can help with that."

"Well then, let's get going." Austin was already pulling clothes on before I even had one leg out of bed.

"Right behind you," I muttered, scanning the floor. I located my discarded clothes from earlier and got dressed as quickly as possible.

Austin stepped into me, smoothing the furrow between my brows with the tip of his finger. He then softly brushed his lips over mine. "Don't worry, whatever it means, we'll figure it out together." He grinned, showcasing his dimples. "I guess now we have to believe we were fated to be together."

I rolled my eyes. "Okay, whatever."

"Try explaining us then," Austin said with a glint in his eyes.

"I don't know, but fate had nothing to do with it. That would imply we don't have control over our destinies."

Austin grabbed my hand, leading me out of the room. "Maybe we don't," he mumbled under his breath.

I sucked in a breath as I prepared to argue, but decided we had plenty of time to discuss our existential beliefs and values later. It simply wasn't the right moment. Plus, there was a chance that I was already leaning more to his line of thinking, but I simply didn't like what it said about my life or the things surrounding it. Was I destined to become addicted to death emotions? As a child, was there nothing I could have done, no path I could have chosen to end up in a different place? Was it an 'all roads end here' situation? Or could it possibly be more of a 'certain things are more likely' situation?

"Austin." Taryn intercepted us in the hallway, forcing me to focus. "I was just coming to get you. Your time's up."

Austin's grip on my hand tightened. "We need to find Cal first."

Taryn frowned, avoiding my gaze. "I'm sorry, you know I don't like this—any of it—but you agreed."

I peered up at Austin's profile, a muscle in his jaw twitching. "What did you agree to, Austin?"

Pushing at his mind, I growled under my breath when he shut me down. *Really, asshat? You really think you can—*

"I'm not free to go, Sam. I'm still … under suspicion."

My annoyance at Austin instantly dissolved into

shock, before morphing into anger. "What? You've got to be fucking kidding me!"

I'd been under the impression that after the conversation Nixon and I had in the hotel room, and with Austin being at the airport to greet me, that Nixon and everyone else had finally come to their senses.

But apparently, I'd been wrong. When Nixon had 'granted' us some time together at the compound it didn't have anything to do with delaying some kind of meeting or debriefing, no. He was giving me the equivalent of a conjugal visit before throwing my husband back under lock and key.

Grinding my teeth together, I glared at Taryn. "Where is he?"

Austin brushed my jaw with a fingertip, gently attempting to turn me towards him, but I wasn't having any of it.

Crowding into Taryn's space, I hissed, "Tell me where the fuck he is right now."

"Calm down, Sam. We need to play ball with Nixon if we're going to have any chance of getting out of this alive," Austin murmured, his tone low and cajoling.

"No! Absolutely not! Nixon is not going to get away with fucking with our lives again!" I yanked away from Austin, focusing on Taryn completely. "Just tell me, Taryn! This is beyond ridiculous!"

Taryn blanched, his gaze darting to anywhere but me. And yet despite his obvious discomfort, he remained mum on the subject of Nixon's whereabouts.

Okay. Fine. I guess we're going to do this the hard way.

Without any of my normal finesse, I dove into Taryn's mind, rifling through his brain in search of the information I wanted, discarding everything I deemed irrelevant. I heard him cry out in pain, but I didn't comprehend it on some level, my task more important.

Strong fingers dug into my shoulders, shaking me roughly, but not enough to deter me from continuing to probe through Taryn's memories.

"Stop! Sam, no! Can't you see that you're killing him? You have to stop!" Austin's desperate pleas finally penetrated, sinking in slowly.

Blinking, I stared down at Taryn's large body crumpled on the floor in front of me. Blood trickled out of his nose, his eyes were rolled back in his head, and he was convulsing like he was having a seizure.

I covered my mouth with a trembling hand. "Oh my God. I didn't mean to! I would never on purpose—" Choking back a guttural sob, I took a step backwards. "I'm so sorry."

Turning slowly to face Austin, I registered his sudden stillness, his gaze fixated on Taryn, a glint of need burning in his azure eyes. I knew with utter certainty that Austin was no longer seeing his friend lying on the ground in front of us, but instead, a possible death that he could use to temporarily satisfy his dark craving—our dark cravings.

"Sam," he whispered hoarsely. "Get help." A fine tremor ran over Austin's body, and he took a step closer to Taryn.

"He doesn't have much longer," his fists clenched at his sides, "get help."

I glanced down at Taryn and then back at Austin. Even I wasn't to the point where I was tempted to feel Taryn's death, and the two of us weren't even close.

Is Austin already more lost than I am?

Dread clawed its way down my spine. I couldn't afford to leave Austin alone with Taryn, and yet if I didn't then Taryn would surely die. I was stuck between a rock and a hard place without a single good option.

I can trust him. I need to trust him.

Finally forcing myself into action, I pivoted and ran as fast as my feet could carry me away from the living quarters and in the general area of the compound. My voice fraught with tension, I called out for a healer or anyone who might be able to actually help.

Nixon appeared in front of me, grabbing my shoulders as I gasped for breath. "Taryn—dying—need help."

Processing everything quicker than I expected, he uttered, "Fuck," before dashing off in the direction I'd come from. As he ran with me lagging behind, he pulled his phone out of his pocket. "We need you, now." He nodded reflexively. "Yeah, now. North wing living quarters, it's Taryn … he's dying."

My vision blurred, and I staggered. Austin was inside Taryn's mind, feeling his death, and he was bringing me along for the ride. But it was different from what I'd experienced with Malcolm, because instead of creepy the sensation was intimate, and I was hit by the overwhelming urge to go to Austin—to be in his arms, to share the experience while skin-to-skin, and to rejoice in having each other while Taryn suffered alone. Nothing mattered anymore beyond getting to Austin.

Pulled by the tractor beam that was Austin, I stumbled blindly down the hallway, my body a secondary focus to what was unfolding within my mind. Idly I registered that I was no longer standing, having dropped to my hands and knees to crawl instead.

Time slowed to a standstill as I struggled towards my destination, finally arriving an eternity later to find an even more shocking scene than I could have expected. Austin was leaning against the wall, his eyes screwed tightly closed, clearly immersed in the death emotions. Cal was crouched over Taryn with a switchblade held to his throat. And Nixon was frozen in place, a blonde girl standing beside him.

"*Austin!*" I shouted mentally, trying to push past all the deliciously intoxicating death emotions to make him understand the full scope of our situation. Slowly his eyes cracked open as he took stock of his physical surroundings. But he remained immobile, unwilling to react.

The cold, hard truth choked me, and I struggled to breathe. Austin wanted Taryn dead. He wanted Taryn dead because he was already too far gone and he cared more about feeding his new addiction than the life of his friend.

My fault. All of this is my fault. I've tainted him just like I was afraid I would.

Cal narrowed his eyes at me, drawing the blade across Taryn's throat. As a scream tore from my mouth, he winked, my dawning horror drawing amusement from him.

Lurching to my feet, I stumbled towards Austin, who had dropped to his knees with a euphoric smile on his face. I shoved my own death craving aside, fear for Austin's safety trumping everything else. I had to protect him—from Nixon, from Cal … hell, even himself. But before I could reach him, Cal swung around and yanked him to his feet before dragging him down the hallway.

Finding the strength, I leapt into the air as if I could somehow tackle them, but Nixon snagged me around the waist, hauling me against his chest.

"No!" I kicked and thrashed. "He's taking him! No! Let me go! He's taking Austin!"

"I'll come back for you," Austin whispered faintly in my mind.

"No!" I screamed. "No!"

They're gone. They're already gone. They—

Twisting in Nixon's grip, I screeched in his face, "Why didn't you stop it? Why the fuck didn't you stop it?" I pummeled my fists against his chest. "And why the fuck weren't your void shields up? Huh? Was it all because you want an excuse to hunt down Austin and kill him? Are you really willing to go that far?"

Nixon blinked. "They were up," he said flatly. "My void shields were up the entire time."

I'M WEAK AND USELESS.

My worst fear had come to fruition. I'd infected Austin with the dark stain that tainted my soul and now it was too late to save him. It was my fault. All of it had been avoidable, and like a complete fool I'd thrown caution to the wind, expecting a different outcome than the one I'd gotten.

I was a hypocrite. Claiming the need to protect him and then exposing him to death emotions the next moment. I suppose on some level I thought Austin was beyond my weaknesses, and strong enough to withstand what I couldn't. But that wasn't a valid excuse because he was only human after all, with the same weaknesses that all humans have.

No. I don't accept it. It can't be too late. Shaking my head, I gasped out on a sob, "He can be helped. He can be saved."

Nixon stared at me, his eyes wide in disbelief. "He let Taryn die. He just stood there, and then he left with Cal."

Both of our gazes masterfully dodged the blood-soaked floor where Taryn's body had been mere moments ago. For some unknown reason, perhaps shock, we lingered there in the hallway where all of it had gone down.

I pressed my fingers into my throbbing temples. "No.

It's not the same. He didn't kill Taryn, Cal did. And he didn't leave with Cal, he was taken."

Slumping against the wall, I sucked in a ragged breath. "Austin was a victim of the circumstances—circumstances that I created. It was me. I just ripped through Taryn's mind like a hot knife through butter. Whatever punishment you deal out to Austin, I deserve the same."

"No." Nixon grabbed me by the shoulders, his fingers digging in painfully as he glared down at me. "What happened … I know you didn't mean it. And you walked away, came to get help. Austin—"

"It's my fault!" I screeched, spittle flying from my mouth. "I'm the one who made him that way! I'm the one who ruined everything! He can be saved! He …" I broke down into sobs again, sagging within Nixon's tight grip, "… can … be … saved." Lifting my gaze, I saw the doubt and denial lingering in his eyes. "You know it's true. I'm the lost cause, not him. I-I'm like Maggie."

"No!" Nixon's voice cracked, and his arms trembled. "You're nothing like her!"

"Stop. You have to stop. You saw me with your own eyes back in Pittsburgh. I was covered in blood, and I didn't care. If you hadn't been so revolted, you could have had your way with me. In that moment, I wouldn't have stopped you. In fact, I would have loved every second of it flying high on those death emotions."

"No." He shook his head, gaze drilling into mine. "That's not how I want you. That's not how I wanted any of this to go down."

Reaching for him, I let my hand fall before making contact. "Then you need to try and make things right." I swallowed around the lump in my throat. "We've all fucked up. Every single one of us, including you, but only you have the power right now to try and fix what you did."

He ran his hands through his hair, tugging. "What do you suggest we do then?"

I straightened, a fresh bout of determination washing over me. *We can fix this—we will fix this. None of this had to end in tragedy like Maggie and Malcolm.*

"We need answers, the same as always. We need to find out what happened to Natalie, and we need to find out about that list. It's all connected, Nixon. You know it is."

"We don't have any leads."

"Yes, we do. We have me."

He snorted. "What does that mean exactly?"

"There has to be a way to unlock my hidden memories. They're already trying to resurface on their own. There has to be a way to help them along."

He crossed his arms over his chest, his gaze darting over my features. "No. It's too dangerous. You could end up like Taryn."

"Then have a healer on hand. I'm guessing that's who that little blonde chick was?"

Nixon shook his head slowly. "She's not as strong as Jessica was, she—"

I threw my hands up in the air, frustration zinging through my system. "It's the only lead we have right now.

We either do it my way or I'll find a probably less safe way to try it."

Nixon's eyes sparked with anger, and I gave him a tight smile. "That's right, you know I'll do it consequences be damned. And you also know there's no real way to stop me."

Nixon turned and stalked down the hallway, a string of obscenities spilling from his mouth.

"I'll take that as you're off to make the arrangements," I called after him.

Him not responding was my affirmation.

Chapter 20

Keeping my eyes closed, I shifted on the overstuffed couch I was currently reclining on. Relaxing didn't seem to be in the cards for me though.

"Stop pacing, you're making me nervous," I hissed in the direction of Nixon's clomping feet.

"Good, you should be nervous." He paused and then cleared his throat. "I don't like this one bit."

"You don't have to like it because I'm not giving you a choice." I slitted my eyes open to peer at Nixon, who was now leaning against the nearby wall with his arms crossed over his muscular chest. His dark hair was in complete disarray as if he hadn't slept in days. For all I knew he hadn't.

Footsteps from the hallway preceded the guest we'd been waiting for. A tall, thin man with salt and pepper hair entered the room, followed by the little blonde healer whose name I refused to remember. It didn't matter that Austin hadn't hooked up with her while he thought I was dead, I still didn't like the way she so obviously wanted him and didn't even attempt to hide it.

Opening my eyes fully, I met the steel-gray gaze of the man who would be helping me retrieve any suppressed childhood memories. He returned my stare with clinical detachment.

Nixon strode towards the man, offering his hand. "Hello, Dr. Litzkin. Thank you so much for coming on such short notice. We—"

"Let's cut to the chase. You didn't offer me much of a choice, did you? Although the amount of money I stand to make from this job definitely softens the blow."

I quirked an eyebrow. Who exactly was this guy if not some part of our team? With his attitude, I wouldn't normally trust him to rifle through my brain safely, but money could be a great motivator, and I was sure Nixon would set it up so that he would only get paid if I came out on the healthy end of the spectrum.

Slapping my hands together, I said, "Well let's get started then. What do I need to do?"

Dr. Litzkin's lips pulled back into something akin to a grin, and I stifled a shudder. "You don't need to do anything. Just sit back and relax. I will do the rest."

"Okay," I muttered as I resumed my reclined position, sliding my eyes shut again. "But—"

I sucked in a sharp breath as my thoughts were ripped from my control, images racing past as if my life was rewinding within my mind's eye. I ground my teeth together while my head pulsed in a rhythm sure to crack my skull open. Abruptly it all went dark. Before I had the chance to question what was happening, a scene erupted before me, shooting me back to the beginning of the memory I'd dreamt.

Leaning over the small hospital bed towards my neighbor, I smiled. "Hi, I'm Chloe, what's your name?" I could feel the boy's worry and trepidation. He didn't like hospitals, and there was something about him that made me want to reassure him.

He blinked his large, luminous eyes and stared back at me. "Hi," he responded shyly. "I'm Kevin."

I plastered my best warm smile on my face, one that I hoped looked like the one my mom gave me often enough. "You know, hospitals aren't that scary, so you shouldn't worry."

He studied me for a moment before saying, "How did you know I'm worried?"

Uh-oh. I slipped up again. *Sometimes I scared people when I knew stuff about their emotions without them telling me. "Lucky guess? So how old are you, Kevin?"*

"Six."

"Me too." I grinned at him. "So, what landed you in here?"

He laughed. "You make it sound like we're in a prison movie or something."

I shrugged. We were both silent a moment, and then he finally answered my question.

"I'm just getting some tests, but you know that probably means I have some kind of cancer."

It was my turn to laugh. "That's just stupid. I'm here for tests too and I know I don't have cancer."

He sat up and stared at me with a very serious face. "I'm making a break for it, wanna come with?"

I was always up for some fun. "Sure," I said.

We slipped out of our beds and crept into the dark hallway. There were no nurses or doctors around as far as we could see, so we dashed from doorway to doorway, making sort of a game out of it.

"So what are we doing exactly?" I whispered to Kevin.

"We're spying ... going to find out if we're all infected with cancer or maybe something worse."

I scrunched my face up at him. "Worse?"

"Yeah, some kind of flesh-eating bacteria that's gonna make us ooze from the inside out."

"Eeeewww ... I'm not oozing."

"Yet," was all he said before dashing to the next doorway.

But something stopped me short. I felt drawn to explore what was in the room I was in front of. I slid inside silently, making my way to the bed by the window. A beautiful boy laid there, the moonlight from the night spilling across his face. His nearly black hair was sticking up in all directions, and he blinked open the bluest eyes I'd ever seen.

"Who are you?" he asked.

I was hit with a feeling of knowing, almost like someone had reached down into me and placed information into my head. "You're going to be very important to me. And I'm going to be just as important to you."

I slapped my hand over my mouth with horror. Why would I say that? It was embarrassing to say such things to a stranger.

He frowned at me. "I know."

Where the memory had halted before when I woke up, this time it continued on.

I peered at him thoughtfully. "What do you know?"

He shrugged. "Not sure. It's like the words just slipped out of my mouth."

His sadness washed over me, yanking me down into the murky depths of his emotions. I was used to knowing what other people felt, but I'd never experienced it so clearly before. I didn't merely feel his sadness—I was now sad, too. "Why are you so sad?"

His eyes widened with surprise. "A-Are you like me?"

I began to fidget nervously. I'd slipped up again, and yet there was something about the hope in the beautiful boy's eyes when he asked if I was like him. Maybe I was, and then maybe I'd actually found someone I could share my secrets with. "Like you how ... sick?" I hedged.

He smiled at me, showcasing a dimple that made my heart speed up. This beautiful boy was definitely my new crush. 'What's his name' from my kindergarten class was old news.

"No, can you feel stuff about other people?"

"Yeah," I breathed.

"And you just sometimes know stuff like about the future?" His face and emotions had morphed into hope. Maybe he had secrets he wanted to share with me, too.

"Well, I don't really know stuff about the future." I shuffled back and forth beside his bed.

"Oh," he said. "But you said we'd be important to each other. That was about the future."

I grinned. "Yeah, I guess it was."

"I'm Alex." He hopped down from the bed, standing only a smidge taller than me, but Mom told me boys were slower developers than girls. I hoped Alex would grow up to be tall so he could be my boyfriend.

"I'm Chloe."

"So, what are we doing?"

"Oh, well, my roommate Kevin and me were going to spy on stuff." I shrugged. "His idea, not mine."

Alex's smile brightened. "I like it, let's go."

He reached out his hand for mine, and I slid it into his. The minute our skin touched, the two of us gasped in unison. My head swam with his thoughts, and I could tell his was doing the same with mine.

We spiraled into darkness together.

"DO *you have any idea what happened?" a male voice asked blandly.*

"It's hard to say exactly. But these two are some of the strongest we brought in, and we were planning on using them for the baselines for the planned experiments," a female voice said with excitement. "Maybe we could hook them up to the scanners and see what happens when they interact again."

"Don't get ahead of yourself, Natalie. Although—"

"Although it's promising, isn't it, David? And to think we stumbled upon her purely by accident."

"Yes, Chloe was brought to our attention by her psychologist, wasn't she?"

"Yes, and we paid her generously enough to keep an eye out for kids like her, but in the end we merely got lucky. Her parents think we're trying to help cure children like her with mental disorders." She laughed. "If they only knew what their daughter really is."

I remained perfectly still as I listened to the conversation. I was scared by what I was hearing and wasn't completely sure why. I didn't trust these two people, not one little bit. I wanted to go home, and I wanted my parents.

"We might actually find what we're looking for, David. This might all work out in the end."

"I hope so, I really hope so. We can't afford to lose the grants, especially when I know we're right. We can duplicate and strengthen the genes these two carry."

"We'll check on them in a bit then. I'm going to gather the equipment I'll need for when they wake up." Natalie's voice grew fainter, signaling she was leaving.

"Mhmm ..." David mumbled as his voice faded as well.

I waited a few minutes before opening my eyes slowly. My heart pounded in my ears as fear ricocheted through my system, making me feel like I was going to throw up. After sliding out of the hospital bed cautiously, I scampered over next to Alex's bed. His eyes were still closed, and his breathing was even. Reaching up to touch him, I stopped myself short as the memory of what happened the last time hit me.

"Alex," I whispered. "Alex, wake up."

"I am awake." He opened his bright blue eyes to meet my gaze. "I'm just better at pretending to be asleep than you." He smirked slightly at me, and I had to fight the urge to punch him. "You don't have to be afraid, Chloe. I'll protect you."

I raised my chin at him defiantly. He really was like me, but I was finding I didn't like it much. "I'm not afraid. And I don't need your protection, I'll protect you."

He grinned. "We can protect each other then. Deal?"

"Okay," I said, mollified.

I shifted from foot to foot, my bare feet cold on the tile floor. Clamping my mouth shut, I resisted the urge to ask him if I could climb into bed with him. Would he think I was a baby? I didn't want to admit out loud that I was afraid even though I knew he'd sensed it since he was like me. And I was nervous at the thought of being so close to him. Maybe when we were older, he'd be like my Westley from Princess Bride, *but not if he thought I was a scaredy-cat baby that he had to take care of. He probably already thought I was a baby though. I could tell he was older than me, at least nine or ten.*

"Come here, Chloe," Alex said, a faint smile touching his lips. "I don't think you're a baby."

My cheeks heated. "I ..."

I was embarrassed, but when he offered me his hand, I took it without thought. Again, like the first time we touched, I slipped into his mind as he seemed to slip into mine. This time, though, it wasn't completely unpleasant. In fact, it was kind of nice to feel so close to someone. I shifted until I was under the covers with him and curled up against his side, my head tucked under his arm. Instead of feeling like a baby, I felt very adult. Maybe Alex really would be my Westley one day.

We fell asleep like that, inside each other's minds and in each other's arms.

YAWNING, *I opened my eyes slowly, liking the feeling of being in Alex's arms and his sleeping thoughts still being connected to my mind. I smiled up at him, lifting my hand to hover over his face. He was so pretty. Much prettier than me. But not in a way that anyone would ever mistake him for a girl like some boys from my school were. He was like an angel—my angel. I felt safe with him, and I liked knowing that he could share my secrets and truly understand. Maybe he would be more than my Westley one day; maybe he would be my best friend. I'd always wanted one of those, but I'd never been able to trust someone all the way.*

"Hey," Alex murmured.

"Hi," I said shyly, quickly dropping my hand back down to my side.

He sat up, and I slid out from under his arm as he looked around the room. "No one came in to check on us? They didn't come back?"

"No, I don't think so."

Alex grinned. "All right then, it's time for us to spy for real this time. You up for it, Chloe?"

I nodded. "Of course."

"Well let's go then." He was already making his way to the door before he finished talking.

I scampered after him, my bare feet smacking the cold floor.

Alex waved me back when he paused to peer out the door. His apprehension washed over me, and he turned back to signal me to stop. My breath caught in my throat, and I stood stock still until he motioned for me to come forward.

I halted right next to him, and he whispered in my ear, "Be quiet and be ready to run back to your bed when I say."

I nodded in understanding and turned my attention to the hallway.

"The first round came back negative," Natalie said, frowning down at something in a folder.

David sighed heavily. "Okay, so we need to step up what we're doing. Push harder. I know we're on the verge of a breakthrough. Jase is coming in with his void abilities. He's one of the most important recent discoveries yet. We might be able to see if there's a drastic difference in him from the others or if it's just another ability attached to the same gene coding. And you were so excited before about Alex and Chloe."

Natalie looked at David and gave him a small smile. "Yes, those two also have some very interesting implications. We need to move them on to more vigorous testing. I think they're better paired than Chloe and Kevin would have been. We'll put him with someone else."

"I'll go prep Chloe and Alex then," David said as he moved towards us.

I didn't even need Alex's signal to make my mad dash back

to my bed. I quickly jumped up and waited for whatever was coming for us.

"It'll be okay Chloe," Alex whispered from his bed.

TERROR SURROUNDED *me from all sides. Internal as well as external screams affronted me. My smaller hand trembled within Alex's larger one. I peered up at his face, his crystal blue eyes taking everything in calmly, but I knew he wasn't as calm on the inside.*

We had been taken to the most horrific place I'd ever been to. It was like a lab on some sci-fi show I might watch on TV. Although the things happening around me would never happen on anything my parents would let me watch. I tried not to stare as a man in a white lab coat made an incision in a young boy's arm who cried out in pain. Beside him, a girl not much bigger than me with dark brown hair sobbed. The lab coat man said something to her, and she cried out, "I can't! I'm trying!" Then the man reached down to make another incision, and the girl wailed, "Noooo! Don't hurt him anymore! I caaaan't do it! I can't! I tried! I'm trying!"

A few feet away in a corner another man in a lab coat was doing something that I couldn't see with two other kids, but I could feel their fear and distress.

"I don't want to be here," I whispered.

Alex squeezed my hand. "We'll protect each other. We have a deal, remember?"

I just squeezed his hand back because I didn't like to lie ...

and I didn't think I could protect him here. This place wasn't right. There were too many dark emotions.

David, the man who brought Alex and me to this place, returned to us, moving us forward with a hand on each of our shoulders. "Don't pay attention to all of that. We're trying to help them, but sometimes the process can be painful."

"Lie," Alex stated. "The only one you're helping is yourself."

Anger rolled off of David with Alex's remark, and I wanted to tell Alex to be quiet. He didn't want to make David mad. I just knew that would be a bad thing.

David's grip tightened on my shoulder and probably on Alex's as well. "This is all just a means to an end. Once we can isolate the gene code that makes those of you like you ... well, the way you are, then we'll be able to make what we need. Why I'm justifying myself to a kid is beyond me," he growled the last part under his breath.

He led us into a small room and seated us both at a long table. I clutched Alex's hand tighter when my eyes landed on a silver screen in front of us. I wasn't sure what it was, but I was suddenly terrified.

"Now," David said, "I'm just going to take some blood samples first."

He motioned for someone, and the woman called Natalie entered the room. She withdrew small amounts of blood from both me and Alex, but I was used to it. I had blood taken almost daily now.

She pulled me away from Alex and led me around behind the silver screen. My eyes widened when I saw the chair with restraints on it and I dug my feet into the ground, tugging to get away. It didn't do me much good though, and before I knew it, I was strapped down in the chair with a gag in my mouth.

"Ready," she called out.

And then the torture began.

None of it made sense to me. Why was I being shown symbols and pictures, but Alex was being asked what they were? And why was I being physically punished if he didn't get the answers right? Why was he being asked about my emotions?

I whimpered behind the gag as Natalie slapped me across the face. I'd never really been hit before, and it hurt in a way I never could have imagined. She had no real compassion for me. I could feel her studying me with cold detachment like I was a lab rat, like I wasn't even human.

"Stop!" I heard Alex cry out. "Stop hurting her! I promised I'd protect her! Please!" Alex sounded younger than he was, and not anything like the stoic protector I'd already come to think of him as.

My scream was muffled as Natalie wretched my finger to the side. I heard it snap. Alex screamed for me. He continued to cry out as my vision darkened and I passed out.

A FEW MONTHS LATER ...

"I don't understand," I sobbed. "Why are they doing this to us, and why are our parents letting them?"

Alex hugged me tightly. "I don't think our parents know, but I know why they're doing all of those things to us."

"Why?"

"They're trying to figure out what makes us tick so they can duplicate it, make more of us that they can use."

"Use for what?"

Alex shrugged. "I don't know, grown-up type stuff. To rule the world or get money ... you know, all the usual."

"But everyone else is gone. They let everyone else go home to their families but us. Why? What's so special about us?"

"I don't know, Chloe. I really don't know." He tightened his grip almost painfully, but I was used to pain by now. "I'm sorry, so sorry."

"For what?" I asked in a whisper.

"I promised to protect you and I haven't been able to."

"But you have protected me the best you can. Alex, you're my best friend and I just don't know what I'd do without you. They would have destroyed me if it wasn't for you."

"You're my best friend, too, Chloe. I'll figure something out. I'll get us out of here eventually, and I promise to keep that promise."

I smiled into his shirt. "I know."

The rest of the memories were jumbled, shaped in pain and terror. But throughout it all, it was Alex and me against the world. It was hard to say how long we were held in that hospital, how many countless experiments and terrors we were forced to face, but Alex and I ... Austin and I had bonded, and I hadn't remembered any of it, and neither had he. Was that why we'd been so inexplicably drawn to each other? Had something deep down in him been waiting for me and not even known it? They say traumatic events can bond people together for life, is that what happened to us? What had they been doing to us exactly? What were they trying to achieve? All I had were guesses.

A flash of Dr. Litzkin's younger face juxtaposed with his current older face appeared in my mind's eye, sudden pain ripping through my skull. And then I was freefalling into oblivion.

Chapter 21

Jolting straight up, I scrubbed a trembling hand through my hair. I hadn't left the room physically, and yet I'd gone on quite the journey. I turned my gaze towards Dr. Litzkin, narrowing my eyes at him. "Well, well, well … It seems as if we've met before," I said drolly.

His elderly face broke into a tight smile. "Yes."

Nixon hurried over to me, concern pinching his features. "Is it over already? How do you feel?"

Without breaking eye contact with Dr. Litzkin, I answered Nixon, "Oh, yeah. It's over. And I remember everything now." I tilted my head at the dear doctor. "What you take away, ye shall giveth back, eh, Doc?"

"What are you talking about?" Nixon asked. He then turned to the blonde healer. "You can go."

She slunk away, not uttering a word or glancing back

once, seemingly intent on escaping the pending situation as quickly as she could.

I met Nixon's troubled gaze as I drummed my fingers along the arm of the couch. "It seems that your man on call not only can retrieve memories, but take them away. In fact, he's the one who suppressed my memories to begin with. How exactly do you know him, Nixon?"

Nixon's right eye twitched. "Natalie used him from time to time. He's very expensive, though, and—"

"Yeah, I bet," I interjected. "That's because I'm guessing Dr. Litzkin is the one who David had on the payroll. I think someone has some explaining to do." I narrowed my eyes at the doctor once again, fighting to suppress my anger. I didn't want to have to hurt him ... at least until I got my answers.

He raised his hands in surrender. "I wouldn't have come and returned your memories if I wasn't prepared to give you the answers you want. This has all gone too far. Lines were crossed and promises broken."

I crossed my arms over my chest and clicked my tongue. "Start talking then."

Dr. Litzkin dipped his chin in acknowledgment of my command. "David and Natalie started out meaning well." He paused to clear his throat. "At least it seemed that way to me."

He hesitated another moment before continuing. "They were under government contract to study and isolate the genetic phenomenon which resulted in people such as us that have special abilities. They wanted to make the perfect soldier, one who lessened the chances of collateral damage and one that would revolutionize the special ops forces as we know them." The doctor's eyes gleamed. "Can you imagine a soldier being able to get in and out, unseen and unheard to take out a target? Or what about our military not even having to fire a single shot at the enemy, to take them down with their minds alone? The possibilities were and still are endless."

When he put it that way, it almost seemed like a good idea. Almost. "What went wrong?"

The doctor frowned, his eyes glossing over. "Most of you weren't strong enough, didn't function well under pressure. There was one exception."

I already knew what he was going to say with the way I was still being targeted. "Me?" I asked, although I meant it more as a statement.

"No."

Shock coursed through my system. *That can't be right. Then why ...*

"Alex, or what you know him by now, Austin."

I shook my head in an attempt to dislodge my confusion. "Then why have I been the one targeted time after time? Why am I the one that everyone—"

Suddenly all the pieces clicked into place, the answer painfully obvious. "Oh my God," I whispered. "They're still trying to use me to get to him. Just like when we were kids. It's because I bonded with him. They're not trying to flip me at all ... but him. It's been about Austin all along."

The doctor nodded. "No one was able to figure out

exactly what caused such a tight bond between the two of you, but—"

"What's he talking about?" Nixon interjected in obvious exasperation. Not that I could blame him. He hadn't been made privy to the information from my restored memories yet and without them, he couldn't fully follow our conversation.

"Come here." I motioned for him to approach me.

I glanced at the doctor. "Hold that thought a second."

Nixon closed the distance between us with two large strides, and I grabbed ahold of his wrist. Shoving all of my new memories into him, I studied his visage as shock, fear, and finally, anger played across his features. When I released him, he took a few unsteady steps backwards before swinging his gaze towards Dr. Litzkin.

"You good?" I asked Nixon.

Without breaking his stare from the doctor, he grated, "Yeah. I'm good."

Dr. Litzkin ignored Nixon and tilted his head to study me. "Interesting, you can still pull from each other's powers."

"What?" Nixon and I said in unison.

"Because of the bond you and Alex shared, the two of you began to be able to pull from each other's abilities. It made him stronger and gave you gifts to use that weren't your own, but the two of you were only children. Now …"

"Now," I continued for him, "we're both stronger and so is our bond."

The doctor nodded again. "Ultimately the operation

broke down. Natalie and David no longer saw eye to eye on the particulars of how to handle things. After several breakthroughs were made, the relationship between them became volatile. Natalie gained her ability and David gained none. David became increasingly cruel, and Natalie, because she became one of us, became empathetic to our special needs. In the end, they struck a deal and went their separate ways."

I pinched the bridge of my nose. For someone who claimed to want to share information, Dr. Litzkin continued to be annoyingly unclear with details. "Okay, that's still being kind of vague. What kind of deal?"

"Natalie could have her operation and continue on, unharassed by David and his team, if Natalie agreed to turn over special cases to him."

"Special cases?" Nixon asked.

"Yes. He wanted any people who he thought might be more inclined to the kind of work he wanted—the latest project he'd been working on before his untimely death—the perfect assassin. Just think, an empath who enjoys killing. There would be no remorse, no lingering feelings of guilt, and that empath could reach in and get any pertinent information from the target as they died. He forced Natalie's hand. She would sacrifice a few to keep the many safe and to keep trying to help in ways that managed to assuage her guilt."

More pieces snapped into the place in the bigger puzzle … finally. "Malcolm, Maggie … me. But what about Austin and the others?"

"Things changed after David's death. Someone new was put in charge. Someone who makes David look soft. His name is unknown because he wants to remain in the shadows, but I've been observing, and his current focus is Austin. He'll do whatever it takes to get him, and it looks like he may have finally reached his goal."

I swallowed around the lump in my throat. "Thanks to me."

Coldly, Dr. Litzkin nodded. "Austin couldn't be reached before you. You're his weakness, the back door into his subconscious. All of it was made possible because of you."

"So Malcolm being sent after me, the bomb, Natalie disappearing, my abduction … all of it was to get to Austin through me? To get him to become addicted to death emotions through me because of our bond?"

"Precisely." Dr. Litzkin nodded yet again. "Austin will be the perfect weapon. An assassin with seemingly limitless mental gifts—he doesn't even know the full scope of his powers yet. There have been many more breakthroughs since you were children, and there is also hope of duplicating Austin's abilities and giving them to others. His only weakness before was all the guilt he carried around with him. By killing his mother, David accidentally put up a roadblock to his own goal. But then another way was found in."

Me. "Why wasn't I found sooner? Why didn't—"

"That part I'm not sure about. Maybe they didn't think the bond would still be there, maybe …"

My mind tripped over a memory. It was the night I thought I'd met Austin for the first time.

"Hear! Hear!" I clinked her bottle with mine and smiled, letting the electric emotions of the people around me seep in and fill me to the brim. In another few minutes, I wouldn't know that the emotions I was feeling weren't mine. It was easier to just let go and stop thinking, at least when the emotions were positive. It was the type of high that no drug could duplicate. But just like with any high, I would suffer doubly tomorrow. I would be left feeling empty and void, worn out. Better make the cake worth the bake.

"Let's dance! They're playing my song!" I said, taking a swig from my beer. Truthfully, I had no idea what song was currently playing, but I already was feeling good, and about to feel better.

"See, I love it when you get like this, Chloe! You're so much fun! So carefree!"

Tristin led the way to the center of the dance floor. Funny how we always seemed to own the place when we were here. We both started moving to the music. Our styles were very different, her a much better dancer than me, but I didn't care, I was having fun. As we gyrated, we laughed at nothing and everything. I reveled in the feelings of excitement, hope, and lust. I could almost taste all of it, sweet and decadent, like a treat I rarely had the pleasure of enjoying. Life was good, at least for the moment.

After a few songs, I was draining the bottom of my beer and in desperate need of a refill. I left Tristin grinding on some guy she'd probably end up going home with despite the fact she'd just met him. But I wasn't judging. Her body, her decision. Still swaying to the music, I fought my way to the sidebar where I waved at Rocco. He nodded, letting me know he'd get me next.

"Let me buy you a drink," a masculine voice rumbled much too close to my right ear, hot breath tickling my cheek. I turned, finding myself face to face with Hundred-Dollar Guy.

Was he following me? Wait, why would I think that? If he wanted to keep the party going after Club Elite, it would make sense that he'd end up somewhere nearby. Even still, something wasn't right. But I wasn't getting a creepy vibe, just a few niggling-doubts accompanied by suspicion.

Reaching into the waist of my jeans, I slid my fingers down my hip to retrieve a twenty, waving it at him. "In a way, you already have."

His azure gaze glinted in the low light as his lips turned up slightly. "That's not what I meant, and you know it."

"Sorry, I don't accept drinks from strangers."

He tilted his head slightly and donned a smirk. "But you'll accept a tip of ninety-four dollars and twenty-five cents from a stranger without any problem?"

"Yep. I was working, that was me getting paid. Totally different." I winked and turned away to wait for Rocco, who was taking too long if you asked me.

"Mmm ... I see. I'm Austin, by the way."

Good for him. I grinned at Rocco as he slid my new beer across the bar. About time. *"Jimmy said to put it on his tab," I called out, and Rocco gave me a thumbs-up.*

"Jimmy can buy you a drink, but I can't?" Austin asked as he followed me towards the dance floor.

I glanced over my shoulder at Austin. He was looking pretty good to me right about now. But I couldn't tell if my reaction to him was mine or if it was the overwhelming lust permeating the club. Feeling good, happy, carefree, and even lustful enough to maybe dance with a stranger was as far as I ever pushed it. "Jimmy's not a stranger. You are."

"I just introduced myself. All that's left is for you to tell me your name, and voilà, we're not strangers anymore."

He grabbed my wrist and spun me towards him as if it were a dance step. My head swam, and I gasped. Every single one of his emotions surged through me as all of mine filled him up, and at the same time he was getting his own emotions filtered back to him through me as I got mine through him ... it was a tangled, bizarre, jumbled loop.

"What the fuck?" he muttered, his eyes wide and transfixed on mine.

"How—what—Don't touch me!" I yelled, stumbling away from him.

I maneuvered in and around people, going deeper into the crowd in an effort to lose him. What the hell just happened? *Was my weird ability going wonky? Or did it have something to do with him? I wasn't going to stick around to find out, that was for sure.*

I made a beeline for the back door, slipping out before Austin or any of my friends spotted me. I paused to breathe in the cool night air once outside, before hastily making my way from the back alley towards my car.

I snapped back to the present with Nixon and Dr.

Litzkin. "The bond never went away. It was merely dormant and all it took was for us to touch again."

When I was reintroduced to Austin, I'd regurgitated the same thing I'd told him as a kid, that we'd be important to each other. As a child it had been a premonition, but as an adult it was a memory of a premonition because Austin and I had already become important to each other, we merely had no memories of our time in the hospital together.

"It seems like we've all been pawns from the very beginning."

"Your lives have not been your own. None of yours." Dr. Litzkin eyed Nixon, who stared back at him with a muscle in his jaw ticking. "Not since you were children. But now you know what you've been dealing with and therefore you can change that once and for all."

"So why are you revealing all of this to us now?" Nixon grated.

"Because I was promised that my son would be left alone if I helped them. That promise was broken."

Nixon's eyebrows shot up. "And who's your son?"

Dr. Litzkin sagged into himself, grief pulling his aging features down. "Cal. Cal is my son."

He waved his hand idly. "Plus, that list, it was of everyone who was part of the experiments done by David and Natalie when they were children. Not everyone had been found. I'll help you in any way that I can, just get my son back before it's too late."

"I want my memories back from that time period, too," Nixon snapped. "I'm going to go bring Tasha back."

I opened my mouth to protest, but then snapped it shut. Nixon had every right to take any means possible to retrieve his memories. It was his mind and his body.

"No need for a healer," Dr. Litzkin called after him as he stepped out the door. "It would only be dangerous if someone else tried to retrieve them. I took them, so it's perfectly safe. Although, there will be some pain as Samantha experienced."

I smiled weakly at Nixon. "You can handle it."

He grinned. "If you can, I know I can."

I wanted to roll my eyes at his bravado, but instead, I took his hand as he settled onto the same couch I'd just been on. I could never be with Nixon the way he wanted, but I was no longer angry with him for what he'd done to me. After all, I wasn't even sure that the decision to steal me away hadn't been planted there by someone else. People in love are easily manipulated. I knew that from first-hand experience.

Chapter 22

"Do you think Natalie's still alive?" I asked as my eyes tracked Nixon's path across the floor, back and forth, back and forth … his anxiety ramping mine up exponentially. I ground my teeth together.

He abruptly halted, swinging his gaze my way. "Of course she is. It's all very clear to me now. She planted the evidence on Austin and set all of this into motion. I'm guessing she'll be making a reappearance soon." He resumed pacing while also running his hands through his hair. "I'm also guessing she didn't count on us getting back our memories because of Dr. Litzkin's interference."

"Stop pacing for fuck's sake!" I snapped. "Just … just sit down." I bit my lower lip and grimaced. "I'm sorry. I didn't mean to yell at you. I'm nervous, and you're making it worse with all your anxious energy."

Nixon stalked over to the couch and perched himself

next to me, covering my hand with his. "Forget about Austin. He's what they've been after—what they wanted from the beginning and now they have him. We'll find a way to break the bond and then …" He turned away from me and shook his head. "I don't know, maybe they'll leave you alone. They have him, they don't need you. Don't let some misplaced childhood affection—"

Yanking my hand away from him, I snarled, "It's not misplaced childhood affection. I fell in love with him as an adult. Maybe the bond drew us to each other, and made it nearly impossible to stay away from each other, but—"

My mind flashed to Austin hovering above me, his azure gaze pinning me in place as he buried himself deep inside me. "No, what developed between us as adults was … is love. There was nothing you could have done to keep us apart. There was nothing anyone could have done. That should make you feel better at least."

I heaved a huge sigh and slumped back into the couch, the overstuffed cushions swallowing my shoulders. "I love him, Nixon. The memories of what we went through together only make me feel it that much more. I loved him in my own way as a child, and then I fell in love with him as an adult. I suppose I was just destined to fall in love with him over and over no matter what I did."

"No. Maybe the bond happened naturally, but everything else was— You both … all of us were pawns!" Nixon's face flushed. "Just fucking let him go, Sam! Even if you can't be with me! Let him go because he's already gone!"

Launching to my feet. I clenched my hands at my sides. "He's not gone! And I'll never let him go! Never!"

Nixon studied me a moment before responding, his voice coming out a low whisper, "So what do you plan on doing then? You going to go join him? Become his partner in crime and just go around killing people—sucking down all their death emotions and fucking after each and every one?"

I slapped Nixon across the face. "Don't you dare."

Not bothering to acknowledge what I'd done, he continued, "I can just picture it now. The two of you covered in blood, naked, and ..." His voice cracked. "Having a grand old time."

I gasped as a piece of a nightmare from not too long ago sprung to life in my head.

"THAT'S RIGHT. *You know I'll always take care of you, Sammy. I love you so fucking much." Austin's voice was thick with love and lust, a beautiful combination.*

Peering down at him as he tugged me towards the ground, shock surged through me. Blood, blood everywhere. We were both completely coated in it. How could I forget?

Despite the circumstances, I still didn't resist as Austin covered me with his body. As he entwined our hands, shifting above me, I turned my head to the right for some unknown reason—coming face to face with brown, lifeless eyes. I screamed as I bucked against Austin.

Tightening his grip on me, Austin murmured, "It'll be okay.

Trust me, Sam, my good Sammy girl."

Unable to return my gaze to Austin's, I screamed again and again as I took in the horror of our surroundings. We were languishing amongst a sea of dead bodies. We were immersed in death. We were a part of it.

And suddenly the death emotions seeped into my consciousness just as Austin plunged into me, my screams morphing from terror to pleasure. I couldn't seem to help it. Nor did I want to deny myself the all-encompassing pleasure.

It was now obvious that the dream was more than just a random nightmare. It was my subconscious trying to communicate with me. Too bad the message sailed right over my head until it was too late.

But it didn't matter, not really. I loved Austin, and I would sacrifice anything and everything for him. "I'm going to save him, Nixon. You'll see."

"No, you won't. You'll lose yourself, just like Maggie, just like Malcolm, and … hell, all of the rest of them." Nixon yanked me into his arms, burying his face in my hair. "I can't lose you. I can't watch you become like that. And—"

"Why did Natalie let us kill Malcolm, and you guys kill Maggie with the deal she had in place with David? That part I don't understand."

"Does it matter? We can't change any of that, and—"

I dug my fingers into his shoulders. "Of course it matters, it's a clue. We just need to figure out what it means."

Nixon's grip tightened around me. "Stop! Let it go!

Please! I'm begging you! I'm fucking begging you, Sam." His warm breath skated along my neck as he sucked in ragged breaths, his chest heaving.

After extricating myself from Nixon, I backed away slowly, swaying on wobbly legs. I was mentally and physically exhausted, adrenaline the only thing keeping me going.

Dropping my head, my hair fell across my face in a curtain blocking my view of Nixon as I strode for the door. But before I crossed the threshold, I paused. "I'm going to try and save him. If I can't in the end …"

Guilt and shame clogged my throat and I swallowed convulsively. "Well, in the end, I guess I'll cross that bridge if and when I get to it. But I'm not letting him go, I'm never letting him go. If he goes down, I'll go down. I don't — I can't live without him. I just can't."

As I slunk from the room, Nixon's response curled into my ears on a whisper, "And I'll never let you go, either."

Why? Why won't Nixon let me go? It just doesn't make sense. At least I knew that Austin loved me as much as I loved him. What was the point of Nixon's devotion to me? I wished for his sake that one day he would move on. But honestly, at the moment, I couldn't bring myself to care all that much. I only had room for thoughts of Austin and how exactly I would pull off his rescue.

Hold on. Just hold on. I'm coming for you.

THAT NIGHT my sleep was filled with Austin. But I was tired of memories, it seemed as if they were strangling the life out of me. I wanted the flesh and blood Austin, in my arms where I could hold and touch him, feel him in actuality and not just in my mind. Despite my desires, though, I was forced to temporarily settle for the past, while I craved nothing but my future.

I stared unabashedly as the soft glow of the Vegas strip illuminated the exquisite lines of Austin's body as he lay stretched across our hotel bed on his back. His muscular chest rose and fell evenly as he slept, his dark hair slightly damp around the edges and tousled in sexy disarray. One arm was thrown over his face haphazardly, his full lips parted slightly making him seem vulnerable in a way that made my heart clench.

I'm married to Austin now. He is my husband, and I am his wife. Who would have thought that would be such an aphrodisiac? Maybe he's ready for sleep, but I sure as hell am not.

Sliding down his body, I ran my fingertips over his warm skin. "Austin," I purred, darting my tongue out to run along the ridge of his cock.

He mumbled something incoherent, not yet waking fully even though the part of his anatomy I was currently focused on swelled and stood to full attention.

Sucking him leisurely, I knew it wouldn't be long before I pulled him from dreamland. Not that he would mind, of course. After all, what straight man would complain about being woken up by a blowjob from his new wife?

Austin's hands found their way into my hair as he groaned. A moment later, his sleep-roughened voice broke the silence. "If this is what marriage means, I could definitely get used to it."

Snorting through my nose, I kept up with my ministrations, adding some hand action into the mix. Austin's hips rose off the bed in an effort to sink deeper into my throat, but I didn't let him. I was currently the one in control.

"Come here, wife. I want inside more than your mouth."

Fisting my hair, he tugged, but I protested his command by gripping him harder.

Fuck, I love this man—my husband. He's so fucking sexy. *And I wanted to wring from him the soft grunts of pleasure he always made when I swallowed him down. Quickening my pace, I swirled my tongue around him as I sucked at the same time. He bucked his hips, tightening his grip in my hair.*

Just when my mouth was beginning to get sore, he swelled that little bit more and spilled over into my throat. He mumbled something that might have been English and then sank back into the bed. When I was sure I'd cleaned his length thoroughly with my tongue, I cuddled under his arm with my head on his chest.

Austin's lips brushed my forehead and his fingers crept along my spine. "Give me a minute and it's my turn," he said languidly.

I shook my head. "No, that was me doing something for you. I—"

Suddenly I was in motion as he flipped me over, pinning me under him. "Did I say I was giving you a choice?" My giggle turned into a moan as he deftly explored my slick folds with his fingers. His grin turned wicked, and his eyes burned like twin blue flames. "That's what I thought. How could my wife say no to me?"

The dream memory shifted, and I was standing in an unfamiliar room that resembled a jail cell, although nicer because it seemed to have a private bathroom. Austin stood in front of me in the same clothes Cal had dragged him off in, his gaze locked with mine.

"Austin!" I threw myself into his arms despite knowing none of it was real. Pressing my face into his chest, I let his scent envelop me in comfort.

He stroked my hair, his grip on me bruising. "Everything's going to be fine, Sam. I know everything that you know … everything."

I nodded against his chest.

"And Nixon's right, you need to let me go."

Shock ricocheted through my system. "What? No! I won't! I can't!"

"I don't want to let you go. But fuck, Sam, everything they've done to you, all your suffering was because of me." He pulled me out of his arms, locking his gaze with mine, his azure gaze shining with grief and determination. "I love you more than fucking anything, which is why I have to do this now. If I don't, there's going to be a time when I won't be able to anymore. I-I'm changing. I can feel it. It's like there's this thing inside of me spreading, like—"

"Like it's a disease contaminating your very soul." I gave him a tight smile. "I know. And it's my fault. We've suffered because of each other. But at this point none of that matters anymore. I'm not letting you go, Austin. I'm too selfish for that."

He made a strangled noise in the back of his throat. "You're too selfish? I think I have that market cornered. I let Taryn die, Sam. Even you had the strength to pull away and I didn't. I wanted it and I enjoyed feeling it. I—"

"We'll find a way to fix you … to fix *us*. Just please, I'm begging you, don't turn away from me. I can handle almost anything except losing you again."

His eyes glazed over, and he turned his head away from me. "Who said I'm giving you a choice? When you wake up you won't remember me."

Terror fisted my heart, constricting my chest. "You can't do that."

Austin's lips curved up into an arrogant smirk, his eyes emotionless. "I can and I will. I just … I had to say goodbye first, I guess for me, really, since you won't remember any of this in the end." His Adam's apple danced in his throat. "Because in my heart you'll always be my wife and the one and only woman I'll ever love until the day I feel my own death."

His lips crashed into mine brutally, his desperation spiking through my veins like a shot of adrenaline, bringing all my senses to full alert. I wrapped my arms around him, trying to hold on, but he slipped through my mind and through my metaphorical fingers like tiny grains of sand.

And then he was gone.

Chapter 23

Groaning, my eyes fluttered open, my pulse thumping painfully against my temples. I was lying on my bed face down, fully clothed. My thoughts were muddled and slow, like they were stuck in molasses.

What the fuck happened? I rubbed my gritty eyes and swallowed, my tongue thick and heavy in my mouth. My mind scrabbled for fragments of something important, something—someone I had to remember … someone extremely important …

Blue eyes flashed in front of me, unleashing the cascade of information I was searching for.

Fuck! That stupid, arrogant ... asshat! Stop trying to make decisions for me!

Anger twisted my stomach, causing nausea to roil my gut. *Does he actually think he can erase himself and everything will be fixed just like that? He's so lucky I love him, otherwise I might be tempted to murder and enjoy his death the next time I see him.*

I supposed his attempt was noble, but fortunately for me, for some unknown reason, the memory wipe didn't stick this time around. Reaching out to Austin, a fresh surge of anger heated my blood when I found him completely closed off to me.

Stupid, arrogant asshole! Snatching up the lamp from the nightstand, I hurled it across the room, the glass bottom shattering against the wall with a loud crash. *How could you, Austin? How could you try to erase yourself from my mind? Will you ever stop running from me to protect me? I don't need your protection. I just need you.*

My door swung open, and Nixon rushed in, his brow furrowed with concern. "What happened?" His gaze zeroed in on the broken lamp and then focused on me. "You do that?"

"You see anyone else in here but me?" Sarcasm dripped from my words. And what was he doing exactly … hanging around outside of my door?

"What the hell for? You scared the shit out of me. I thought there was something actually wrong."

I threw my hands in the air. "There is."

His eyebrows crept up his forehead. "What?"

"Austin, of course."

Nixon blinked rapidly and then cleared his throat. "Austin?"

"Yes, Austin. My husband. You … don't remember?"

The blank look on Nixon's face confirmed what I should have already realized.

"Of course he fucking did!" I spat. "He erased himself from your mind. Why would I expect anything less from him?"

My movements jerky as I fought the urge to break something else, I strode over to Nixon. "This is going to hurt."

I pressed my fingers into his temples roughly, releasing my memories of Austin across my subconscious. I knew from experience that it would be enough to trigger his own past with Austin. Plus, apparently, I could pull on my dear husband's powers. Perhaps that was the reason why the asshat couldn't erase himself from my mind. Although technically he'd pulled off the little caper for all of about five minutes. But now wasn't the time to focus on the reasoning why, not when there were more pressing matters at hand.

Grimacing, Nixon pulled away from me and slumped down on the edge of the bed, his eyes sliding shut. "You should have just let me forget. Hell, it was your chance to let it all go. Why the fuck couldn't you, Sam?"

I gritted my teeth against the onslaught of anger, managing to sound somewhat civil when I responded. "I've already told you why. I'm not explaining myself again."

He nodded slowly as he eyed me warily. "I suppose you have a plan?"

I snorted. "Don't I always?"

He grunted. "Care to share?"

"It's pretty simple. I'm going to track down Austin and save the day."

Hmmm ... Maybe I'm sharing a bit of Austin's arrogance along with his powers.

Nixon folded his arms over his chest and gave me a familiar look of doubt. "Yeah, and how exactly do you plan on tracking him down?"

Not wanting to meet his gaze, I flicked mine towards the door. "I have a feeling there's going to be a trail of dead bodies to follow."

My words hung heavily in the air as I stalked from the room.

AFTER A QUICK BUT EFFICIENT SHOWER, I fired up my laptop to do some simple recon on Austin's whereabouts. My gaze almost immediately snagged on a recent headline, and I quickly scanned the article.

Second body found within twenty-four hours in McLean, Virginia. The local inhabitants fear the worst, a serial killer, but investigators say it's too soon to make that call. Michelle McCannon, 24, and Leslie Reynolds, 32, were the confirmed victims, both had their throats cut ...

My fists curled against my keyboard as dread pooled in my stomach. I couldn't bear to read the rest. I knew it was connected to Austin. The real question was: Were these two murders committed by Austin or were they done to let him feel their deaths? If it was the latter, then there was still hope. Because it was one thing to kill the deserving, like serial killers, rapists, etc, but two seemingly innocent women?

I nibbled my thumbnail. *No. There's no way he fell that far that fast. It's only been forty-eight hours since he was taken. Maybe under the right circumstances he could do such things, but not so soon, absolutely not. He's stronger than that.*

Nixon thundered into my room, his emotions dark and snarled.

I glanced up from my computer screen, scowling. "I'm guessing you already read about the two dead girls? They haven't even left Virginia."

Coming to stand directly in front of my laptop, he glared down at me. "I don't suppose you've decided to give it up yet? I mean, it's obviously a trap … you know that, right?"

Crinkling my nose, I quickly shut my laptop. I'd found what I was looking for, and beyond that, I had better resources at my fingertips. "Yeah, I know. And no, I already told you I'm not abandoning him."

"And I guess it's also useless to point out … again … that it's what Austin wants. He tried to save you from this, Sam. He knows what it'll cost you."

I stood and pushed past Nixon, checking him hard with my shoulder. "Don't care."

He let loose a long sigh. "Fine. Then you already know I'm going with you."

"Yeah, yeah, I can't seem to escape you any more than I

can my shadow." I jerked my head in the direction of the door. "I'm going to the crime scenes to see if I can pick up any death emotions from those two women. If Austin thinks I don't remember him, he won't be careful and that might help us track him."

"So, you plan on tracking him just like any other—"

"Don't say it," I hissed.

But the label of *serial killer* hung in the air, dark and ominous, ringing in my ears as if he'd shouted it directly into them.

Chapter 24
NIXON

What do I have to do to get her to let him go, for fuck's sake?

Premonitions are never reliable. They constantly shift, leaving me to scramble for the best possible outcome from the shitty options I usually had. Sam made it even more fucking difficult though. Most of the time when she was involved instead of a gentle shift, the possible futures I could see did one eighties, spinning in the opposite direction. I loved her, and yet she made me want to pull my goddamned hair out sometimes.

I'd done everything in my power to prevent us from arriving exactly where we now were—standing firmly in Sam's darkest timeline, leaving me with very little recourse.

I'm going to have to let her track him, find him. Fuck.

I should have killed Austin years ago, but then I would never have found Sam to begin with. I foresaw an easier path to getting him to let her go after the initial infatuation though, but then he'd gone and fell in love with her, the fucking asshole. I couldn't deny it any longer, not after he revealed his birth name to her, along with his shocking faithfulness even when he thought she was dead.

Yeah, I should have killed him years ago, but I didn't want his blood on my hands. Plus, I'd held onto the hope that they'd eventually go their separate ways, Austin following his usual M.O. of bailing when he got bored … then she would finally be mine. Things didn't pan out that way though. And I'd suffered through their relationship, me, unable to deny her anything she desired, even if it was that scumbag. At one point, there had been futures where Sam and I had ended up together, but now … now—

I just need to try fucking harder to make her mine. Do whatever it takes.

Sam had become my obsession, my reason for everything. And all it took was a glimpse of her in a vision —of the life we could have together—and I knew I would never crave another woman like I did her. Granted, as a ten-year-old kid I didn't quite understand the gravity of what I would one day feel, but it was those images of her that kept me going through the years of torture, and I one day matured into those emotions.

There's no fucking way, after everything I've done and gone through, that I'll let him have her now. She's mine. Not his. Never his.

When she finds him, I'll steal it all from him—his gifts, his memories, and his mental bond with her. And when I have it all, maybe I'll let him live. After all, we were friends once.

At least I finally had the answer to the pull she felt to him, and why she couldn't let him go. I would have preferred getting her a different way, a more honorable way, but ultimately, I didn't care how I got her just as long as she was mine in the end.

I'd reside in hell for her, and if she needed death, I'd give it to her. Because it won't be Austin inside of her reveling in the aftermath of a killing, it will be me, and my name will be on her lips as she screams her release as if he never existed.

Chapter 25

"She didn't see anyone standing in the kitchen when she returned home. It was dark," I murmured. "She thought the house was being robbed. She cried out that he could take anything but—no, they—there's more than one person here and they're taking her. She's terrified and isn't sure what to do. She read somewhere that when someone tries to take you, your best chance for survival is to fight before they get you to a second location. So she struggled, bit, kicked … too strong! No! Take anything you want … just leave me, leave me alone! Everything went dark."

My own breathing echoed in my ears as I focused more intently in an attempt to garner more information. "She awakens to darkness again. Her arms are bound, and there's a pinch at her throat. Nooo! It's a needle. She doesn't want to …"

I skittered over the remnants of Austin slipping in to

feel her death, his essence hugging me within the warm embrace of his dark and seductive thoughts. They curled into my ears with the low timbre of his voice and swam through my brain, caressing my insides. Goose bumps erupted along my flesh as I shivered with delight.

The woman's fear and regret wound through Austin's system, feeding his new addiction. He'd never been so happy … no, happy wasn't the right word. Relieved—yes, relieved—he'd never felt so relieved to be alive. Her death was making him hard, and with that fact guilt and shame punched him in the gut … and yet an image of me flashed across his mind. He wished, again much to his complete and utter shame, that I was there with him, sharing in her death so that we could turn to each other when it was over, to revel in life after experiencing death. He would take me from behind, his fingers sinking into my flesh as he—

I shook my head. *No. Stop. Clues, I need clues to find him.* But there was nothing beyond Austin drinking down the delicious death emotions while he pictured all the wicked things he wanted to do to my body.

Fuck. I want that. So badly. The ghost of his presence held me in thrall as I was carried along in the remnants of his fantasy. I could almost feel him grip my hair in his fist, tugging just the way I liked as he slammed into me from behind. Slick with need, I trembled—desperate to make it real—needing for it to be real.

My eyes snapped open, and I lurched forward as Nixon dropped his void shield, effectively ripping me out of my own perverse thoughts. He reached for me, but I waved him off, clutching the edge of the stainless-steel table where the body was on display for us. The freezing air in the morgue sent a sudden chill through me down to my bones and I shuddered.

Gritting my teeth, I muttered, "No clues."

I pressed my shaky hands into my thighs. I'd been lost for a few moments, my dark urges undeniable even when facing the mere residue of them combined with Austin's enjoyment. My desire to feel death with him was something I couldn't bear to face at the moment. Because if I examined that festering kernel of truth then I would also have to acknowledge how easy it would be to simply go to him. To surrender myself to whoever took him so that I could be used, too. None of it would matter anymore. I would do anything, be anything, as long as I got to be with the man I loved.

No, no, no ... I will save him, not give myself over to the same fate. I refuse.

Nixon barked out a humorless laugh. "No clues? Really? But he was there, and you both enjoyed that, didn't you?"

I whirled to face Nixon. "Just leave it alone."

"You were smiling. Did you know that? You were smiling while you felt her death," he waved his hand at the body, "and you said his name." He shook his head. "No, that's not right. You moaned his name." His expression hardened. "So, did he kill her himself, or was she merely killed for his enjoyment?" He snorted. "Not that you'd admit it if your precious Austin is officially killing for fun now. Let's not kid ourselves."

"You know what I'm capable of—what we're both capable of now. So why are you acting so surprised? It's not the first time you've been front row to witness my enjoyment of death either." I drummed my fingers along the metal table. "He didn't kill her though. Not that you'll believe me since you always want to think the worst of Austin."

Why did Nixon insist on inserting himself into my mission, to supposedly help me, when all he did was antagonize me the entire time? He needed to pick a lane at some point. Did he love or hate me? Of course, I knew love and hate were separated by a very thin line sometimes. Perhaps Nixon's love for me was toeing that line and he'd grow to hate me eventually. I knew it'd be the least I deserved, and then maybe he could move on. I could take solace in his hatred if he could find happiness with someone else. But I couldn't afford for him to hate me just yet, at least not until he helped me get Austin back.

Nixon glowered at me. "Fuck, all right, forget I said anything. You want to see what you can get off of the other body?"

I shrugged nonchalantly, but anticipation was already winding its way through my system, causing me to tremble. My eyes glazed over as Nixon reached his gloved hands over to pull the drawer open, and I was catapulted into a memory of my time with Malcolm.

Malcolm's taunting laugh ricocheted inside my skull. "Every time, Sam, every time."

And with that, I was no longer aware of my body's surroundings because I was seeing out of someone else's eyes.

Dirty fucking bastards double-crossed me. I should have known. I should have been more cautious. Shoulda, coulda, woulda—didn't—fuck. My father always said my ambition and lack of scruples would be the end of me one day. Fucking old coot, guess he was right. What the hell is this sick fuck waiting for? Why doesn't he finish the job instead of leaving me here paralyzed? I can't move a damn muscle. We both know he's going to kill me, so why doesn't he just get it the fuck over with?

"Ready, Sam? This one is going to be a fast high."

Shit, that's a big gun. I hope this doesn't hurt too much. Fuck, why doesn't he just do it already? Why the fu—

The click of the hammer was the only distinguishable sound before everything exploded in a wash of red. I squeezed my eyes shut as I became aware of my own body again. Goose bumps erupted across my skin, and my breaths were quick and shallow like I had just sprinted up a few flights of stairs. The familiar euphoria pumped through my system, leaving me floating in its bliss. The death that both Malcolm and I had just experienced was a shock to my system. The suddenness of it so powerful, so—

Feverish lips crashed into mine as a large, solid body lifted me and pushed tightly against me. Instinctively, I wrapped my legs around that body, not even bothering to open my eyes, grinding myself against the source of my newfound pleasure. The death's euphoria only served to heighten all of my senses, and my nerve endings danced with anticipation of what would happen next.

Austin's image danced through my mind, his piercing azure gaze filled with love and devotion as he stared down at me.

My eyes flew open, and I registered Malcolm's pale face so close it was a blur. Bile climbed into my throat as I wrenched myself abruptly away, shoving at his chest. "What the hell do you think you're doing?"

Blinking his doe-like eyes, he slid reluctantly away from me. "I-I—" he stammered before regaining his composure. "I needed to share the aftereffects with someone, and you're as good as anyone." He shrugged before donning a signature smirk.

Shuddering with revulsion, I wiped my lips with the back of my hand demonstratively. "You mean like you used to with Maggie?" I bared my teeth at him. "So sorry. Just like her, I'd rather have Austin."

I shuddered, revulsion seeping into my pores. The memory was obviously conjured by my psyche for a reason. How would I cope with the knowledge that Austin's need could possibly push him to have sex with someone else? *Hell, Malcolm and I hadn't even liked each other, and it would have been so easy for both of us, if I would have let myself—*

No. I couldn't even finish the thought.

Stop it. That's the last thing you need to be thinking about now. And yet … yet … my gut roiled, raw possessiveness slamming into me like a ton of bricks. *I'll murder anyone who touches him with my bare hands. And that's a death I will enjoy like no other.*

Gritting my teeth, my gaze found its way to the woman's corpse lying on the table in front of me. But I no longer cared who she'd been or how she died, only if she held any clues as to where my husband was. "Drop your shield, Nixon." My fingers gripped the cold metal to the point of numbness.

His void wall fell away, and I dove into the death emotions, gasping when I was jolted by some kind of barrier. When I attempted to push through it, a sticky film clung to me, attaching a fragment of thought. "Sam … Sam … Sam … Sam …" I registered my own voice mumbling, over and over, as if—

Shit. Of course. The woman's death emotions had already been sucked dry, Austin's enjoyment of them the only thing lingering. More specifically, he was flying high on her death, all the while imagining us exploring each other carnally.

No. But wait. Did he remove the death emotions, or did someone else? It didn't make sense that he would only wipe the one death scene but not the other. So I kept searching, my lips forming my name over and over.

Nothing. Nothing. Nothing. Why can't I find a scrap of anything? But I'm not giving up, not letting go. I have to find something.

Nixon's void wall sliced between me and the remnants, causing me to stagger back in frustration. "What the hell? Did I open my eyes or give you any other indication to let you know I was ready for you to do that? I wasn't done yet!"

His nostrils flared. "You repeating your name over and over like that was a good enough sign for me. Plus, it was getting kind of creepy."

I hit my fists against the table, the metal reverberating loudly in the otherwise silent room. My upper lip curled even as I bit my tongue to keep myself from saying something I'd regret—something that would make things more difficult for me to convince Nixon to keep helping me. Sure, we'd fought before when working together. The biggest difference now was that there would be no hot make-up sex between us to smooth things over since I was no longer under the mistaken impression that he was my husband. Although I'm sure I wouldn't have to twist Nixon's arm if I wanted it, husband or not.

Closing my eyes, I counted to ten slowly. When I was done, I met Nixon's gaze, hoping I didn't seem as pissed as I still felt. "Fine, whatever. I guess these two are a dead end, literally."

"There'll be more though," Nixon stated blandly. "Maybe—"

I kicked the leg of the table, grimacing as pain shot up my shin. "Why was this last one cleaned of her death emotions but not the other one? If Austin thinks he erased himself from my memory, then—Fuuuuck."

How could I be so obtuse? Nixon smirked at me, letting me know he'd already arrived at the same conclusion. Austin had begun cleaning up the death emotions so no one could track him down … just like any other serial killer would if it was within their power. But none of that mattered at the moment. The pressing issue was finding out the end game. Dr. Litzkin had claimed Austin was wanted because he would be the perfect assassin. If that was the case, then he wouldn't be knocking off random people whenever he felt like it, he'd have a hit list or a target. Unless whoever was in charge of that operation was anticipating Austin's need to amp up the number of killings and was going to look the other way when it came to those inevitable extracurricular activities. I'd always suspected that Malcolm's handlers turned a blind eye when he'd done the same rather than simply being oblivious. Now I had confirmation of that theory.

"Sooo … what's the next step in your oh-so-brilliant plan?" Nixon's voice was steady but there was no hiding the sarcasm in his tone.

I whirled on him again, stalking towards him. "You are trying to push all my buttons, aren't you?"

Nixon's eyes widened as he took a step back. "Actually, I'm not. I'm trying really fucking hard not to pick a fight with you."

"Yeah, from where I'm standing, it doesn't really seem that way."

Nixon continued to retreat until his back smacked against the far wall. Behind us, both murder victims' bodies remained exposed on their individual drawer tables. I should have reconsidered my actions in respect for the dead, or even for the coroner who was waiting outside. Unfortunately, I couldn't seem to rein in my temper.

As soon as I was close enough, my palm connected with Nixon's cheek, but before I could repeat the motion, Nixon grabbed my wrists, encasing them with his fingers like handcuffs. He then yanked me into his chest, his hot breath fanning over my face. "Knock it off. I'm tired of being your emotional and physical punching bag. We're not together anymore, so you lost that right."

"You've got to be fucking kidding me," I hissed. "Did you really just say that? We were never actually together. I just thought we were, and you were lying to yourself." Thrashing violently within his grip, my forehead connected with his lip.

Nixon's grip on me tightened. "Stop acting like a five year old for fuck's sake. Did you forget where we are? This doesn't look very professional."

My gut twisted as the fire in me fizzled. He was right. I wasn't acting the most mature at the moment. Stilling, I flicked my gaze away from his. After a few heartbeats, Nixon released my hands, and I lurched away from him, turning my concentration to straightening my clothes.

He's right. But I'm not admitting it out loud. No way in hell. And I don't care how immature that makes me either. As an empath, I would always default to my emotions, but lately, with all the stress I'd been under, it was as if I was running purely on instinct, all logic having taken an extended vacation. I needed to get my shit together, but I also knew that until I found Austin that was extremely unlikely.

Narrowing my eyes at Nixon, I ocularly informed him that he wouldn't be getting an apology from me, even if I knew I was in the wrong.

Reading me loud and clear, he scowled as he skimmed his index finger gingerly over his already fat bottom lip. "Ready to go?"

"Yes." Shoving past him, I hurried into the hallway. There, the coroner waited impatiently, a scowl of his own marring his pale unlined features.

"Well …" He pushed off the wall and met my gaze with challenge. "Find anything I missed?"

Arrogant asshole. "No," I snapped.

The coroner's lips curled into a smug grin. Biting the insides of my cheeks, I battled my desire to start a fight with him, and instead whirled in the direction of the exit. As I made my escape, the low tones of Nixon's voice intermingled with the slightly higher one of the coroner as they discussed mundane case facts. I didn't have time for the idle chitchat though, not if I was going to track down Austin before it was too late. If it wasn't already.

Chapter 26
NIXON

I was apparently going to have to leave a trail for Sam to find Austin. I wasn't expecting the part where he'd wiped the second body clean of death emotions. I'd miscalculated and thought there'd be more time before his paranoia about being tracked ramped up. Although, he's always been on the skittish side. Still, it was sloppy of him to leave her name like that. If he had been successful in erasing her memories of him, that little slip-up would have been a dead giveaway that something was wrong once she found her name imprinted on the body. And he knows how she's like a bulldog when she latches onto an idea.

Unless … *Fuck. Does he know?*

Sometimes I didn't give Austin enough credit for being observant, and I knew, just like me, he kept the extent of his abilities under wraps. I had no clue how far his powers had advanced. Maybe the whole erasing him from her memory was just a ploy. That would explain why it didn't stick with her. Perhaps he wanted her to track him down, but for what purpose? Did he want her to join him, or did he think she could save him?

He's seriously delusional if he thinks I'm going to let either of those things happen. I was simply going to have to step up my game. When Sam asked how far I'd be willing to go for the one I loved … she really didn't know what she was asking.

Chapter 27

Nixon was M.I.A. when I sought him out earlier. I couldn't fathom why he would disappear when we had such important matters at hand to deal with. I needed to put together a team to help track Austin down, but with the way Taryn had been killed and Austin taken, well … no one besides Nixon wanted anything to do with me. But since Nixon was still technically in charge in Natalie's absence, he could force people onto the team.

Agitated, I paced outside of Nixon's room for a while before settling on the floor directly across from his door. *Where the hell is he? Seriously …* After what seemed like an eternity of waiting, I began to doze off, my head lolling against the wall.

My thoughts, of course, kept circling back to Austin, and somehow in my semi-conscious state, I slipped right past his mental shields, plunging into the icy depths of his mind. But unlike other times when I'd connected with him, I shrunk my presence down into a tiny ball, being as silent and still as I possibly could, hoping to escape his notice. Only in this state did I have any hope of garnering information and clues without his interference.

"No," Austin growled. "I won't." His gaze swung down to a bound and gagged white woman of undetermined age, although she couldn't have been more than forty. His head snapped to the side as someone's fist connected with his jaw. Spitting blood, he stared up at his tormentor with defiance. "I said no." It was a man I didn't recognize, but I picked up that his name was Matt. He was medium height, muscular, with a shaved head and pale skin. He was definitely ex-military in some capacity.

Matt ground his teeth together in frustration. "I thought you liked this kind of thing? I thought you would want to feel her die?"

"I'm not a killer. I can't help slipping in when they're already dying, but I won't take her life. It's different." I could feel the desperation in Austin. He was trying to resist; he refused to allow himself to cross that line. His mind suddenly flashed to Taryn, his body crumpled in the hallway, and that seemed to strengthen his will.

"It's only a matter of time," Matt said. "Right now we're doing the dirty work for you and you're getting your fix, but what happens when no one is willing anymore?"

Panic erupted inside of Austin, but he tamped it down. "I'm too strong for you to break. I'm down right now, but I'll be making a comeback real soon."

He grinned at Matt, and Matt hit him again.

"Your arrogance is going to be the death of you one day."

"Yeah, my wi—ife ... doesn't like it either." Austin's voice cracked and his emotions swung to sadness.

I wanted to reach out to comfort him, to tell him I was coming for him, but I couldn't risk it.

"Wife, huh? I wasn't informed you were married. Why don't you tell me a bit about her?" Matt's eyes gleamed, and anger tore through Austin.

"Don't even think about her! I'll fucking kill you!" A similar feeling to the one I got when I was furious, probably because it wasn't even my ability, ripped out of Austin.

I expected to see Matt crumple in pain, but instead, the woman on the ground cried out behind her gag. She arched up and began to seize.

Matt laughed. "Whoops, it looks like you're going to be the one to kill her after all."

Austin resisted for longer than I would have been able to, and when he finally slipped into her mind to feel her death, I hit the eject button on my end, hurtling my consciousness away. It was more difficult than I thought it would be to resist, and I was left empty and cold, my entire body trembling in withdrawal. But I was also filled with guilt and anguish. I'd done that to Austin—the man I loved. If I hadn't become addicted to death emotions, if I hadn't been so weak, then none of this would be happening. It all went back to my time with Malcolm.

"Do your worst. I'm not afraid."

He clicked his tongue. "Oh, Sam. But you are. I can taste your fear like sweet, sweet wine aged to perfection."

My eyes widened slightly, which brought a small smile to his lips.

"What? You haven't figured out that I'm an empath, too?"

"B-But ... how can you kill the way you do? How can you do all those things?"

Malcolm's eyes glinted with amusement. "My dear Sam, I like how it feels to walk beside someone in death, to know their last thoughts, to feel their last breath. And then, when their heart stops beating, when their eyes have seen their last image ... I walk away more alive than when I started. I walk away having felt death, yet in a way, transcending it. It's even better than sex."

"Then you haven't been doing it right. Sex, that is."

"Enough," he snapped. "You're trying to distract me, stall me. Time to get down to business."

I fought with everything I had left to keep him from sliding into my mind again, to stop the murky sludge of his presence from mingling with my thoughts, moving around in my head, but I didn't have much of my shields left, and even if I did, I wasn't sure I could keep him out. He was too strong.

I screamed until I couldn't scream anymore.

MALCOLM HAD BEEN RIGHT. I should have been afraid ... very afraid. He'd broken me down and reformed me in his image. At that time in my life, I couldn't even wrap my brain around the concept of enjoying death emotions.

And now … well, now I was just like him and so was Austin. Malcolm may have been rotting in hell, but his goal had been accomplished despite that fact. He'd ruined Austin and me, not our relationship exactly, but us, who we once were. Sometimes you don't know who you really are, until you lose that person. I was like two separate people … Chloe and Sam. Chloe was dead, and Sam had become something—I wasn't even sure what she was. Or maybe she was still becoming whatever she was destined to become? That was the most horrifying possibility of all.

"Did you miss me?" Nixon's deep voice dripped with sarcasm. He stared down at me, his eyes scanning me briefly before he offered me his hand.

Brushing it away, I clambered to my feet on my own. "Where the hell were you? I've been waiting here for hours."

"I had business to attend to," he snapped, averting his gaze. With a grunt of annoyance, he stalked into his room.

I rushed in after him, nervous energy zinging through my system. "We need to put together a team to track down Austin. We can find him in no time if we do. I don't know why I thought I could do it all on my own."

Nixon pulled off the thermal, long-sleeve T-shirt he'd been wearing and reached into his closet for a clean one. My eyes narrowed as they snagged on the large, dark brown stain in the center of his soiled shirt. I stepped closer, hunching down nearer to the ground to get a better look. "Hey, what's that on your shirt?"

"None of your business," he muttered as he snatched it

from the ground and balled it up before stuffing it aggressively into his hamper.

"What's going on with you?"

His shoulders tensed and he stared straight ahead, refusing to meet my gaze. "What? I'm not allowed to get cranky when I've had a bad day? Do I have to be Mr. Perfect for you and give you whatever you want even though we're not in a relationship anymore?"

"I didn't say that, I just—"

"And do you mind getting out of my room? Unless you want to watch me get naked? I know you used to enjoy the show."

I opened my mouth to hurl a retort at him, but his hands went directly to his pants, the zipper whizzing down without preamble, so I hightailed it to the door instead. Nixon was calling my bluff, and I wasn't about to play games with him when he was in such a foul mood.

As soon as I stepped into the hallway, the tiny blonde healer came hurtling around the corner and nearly knocked me over with how fast she was going.

I scowled down at her, struggling to remember her name.

"Where's Nixon?" she demanded, worry etched into the lines of her face.

"In his room." I motioned to the closed door. "But he's getting dressed, so you better give him a minute."

"That didn't take long, did it? I knew you were a piece of work, but Austin hasn't even been gone more than a few days." Her peach-glossed lips twisted into a sneer. "And to think he could have had me."

I knew it! She fucking wants my husband! That part I couldn't exactly fault her for, especially since even Austin had thought I was dead, but who the hell did she think she was making judgments about the complicated situation that was me, Austin, and Nixon?

Calm down. Ignore her. She is nothing to you. I closed my eyes and counted to ten.

But really, who the fuck does she think she is looking down her nose at me? She knows nothing about what Nixon did to me or what Austin and I went through to—

No. Stop. It doesn't matter what she thinks.

I tried counting to ten again.

One ... two ... three ... Austin is mine and she needs to keep her comments to her damn self.

Stop.

One ... two ... Austin is mine!

Yep, so not working.

Anger sizzling through my veins, I exploded into motion, grabbing a fistful of her hair as I pressed her back into the wall with my forearm under her chin. "I'd watch what you say to me. Feeling your death, especially the regrets about my husband *not* fucking you, would be very enjoyable for me."

Her pupils dilated with fear as she struggled against me. "Nixon would put you down if you hurt me. He'd—"

I pushed against her throat, choking off her words.

"He'd what?" I laughed. "You're dumber than you look if you actually believe that. So you better—"

Nixon's door flew open, slamming against the wall. "Let her go, Sam." He sighed heavily. "What is it with you and healers anyways?"

"Apparently they're all idiots," I said as I reluctantly stepped away from her.

"Just … just go in my room, Sam, please. And I'll handle this." Nixon scrubbed a hand down his face, his exasperation evident.

"Fine, whatever." I waved my hand dismissively behind me as I sauntered into Nixon's room, kicking the door shut behind me.

Nixon's low, cajoling tone interwove with what's-her-name's higher-pitched annoying voice as I strained to hear what they were saying. But since I couldn't quite make out any actual words, my attention quickly veered towards the ripe opportunity presented to me by being alone in Nixon's room. We'd been faux married for years, and with the return of my memories he'd become a stranger of sorts, and my curiosity about him was piqued, especially with the chance to snoop.

Casually moving in a small circle while sweeping my gaze over the sparsely furnished room, my gaze snagged on his tiny wooden desk. I slid into the creaky computer chair and pulled open the large drawer on the right. I found most of what one would expect—post-it notes, pens, paper, random receipts, scraps with Nixon's messy handwriting scrolled across them, and ... a stack of pictures of Nixon and me together.

I wanted to ignore them. After all, our entire marriage had been one big lie. However, I couldn't seem to force myself to focus on anything else. My fingers gingerly brushed over the glossy photos as I lifted them from the drawer to study. The first was of Nixon and me out at some bar. I had the glassy-eyed gaze of someone who'd had too much to drink as I beamed up at Nixon and he smiled at the camera. The second picture was of me curled up on the couch in the house we used to share, sleeping with my mouth slightly open. A frown tugged my lips down. I'd been unaware of more than just Nixon taking a picture of me asleep. My entire past was hidden from me by the one person I was supposed to trust more than any other, and yet ... we looked so happy. I thought we were happy.

I dropped the pictures back into the drawer and slammed it shut. Nixon lied to me and stole my past, all so he could pretend to be my husband. That was the truth of the matter. If he'd just wanted to save me, like he'd claimed, there was no need to essentially take Austin's place in my life. There would have been better ways to go about helping me. Instead, under the grandiose banner of love, he tinkered with my memories and stole my life. Could I do something as depraved as Nixon, all the while lying to myself, if Austin loved someone else? What if Austin was an ex-boyfriend and he moved on and I didn't?

Would I be capable of going to such lengths for my one-sided obsession?

Nixon hasn't given up yet. I froze, the realization painfully obvious. *But of course he hasn't.* Deep down, I already knew that, but didn't want to consider the true implications. He'd—at every turn—tried to get me to walk away from Austin, and he would have killed Austin if …

What else is he willing to do? What lines won't he cross?

My adrenaline spiked as sudden suspicion alighted within me. Could he have killed Natalie and somehow procured her approval for him to be in charge before he made that move? I mean, I had accused him of that on our trip to Ohio, but it was nothing more than that … an accusation. I didn't actually believe he was capable of such a thing. On some level, despite his lies, I believed him to be an essentially good person. But now … now …

Did he plant the evidence that could have ultimately ended Austin's life? Why was I blindly trusting the man who stole me from Austin? Why did I think he was good at his core despite his obsession with me? And why didn't he share anything about the memories Dr. Litzkin had returned to him? What other things was Nixon hiding from me?

Panic swirled and crested within me, causing my pulse to quadruple in time. *What if Nixon isn't who I think he is at all? What if no one is?* It was my fault for letting myself trust him again. I'd been suspicious and hadn't trusted him at all, and then I'd just fallen back into old habits because … why? I wasn't sure, but I had. Perhaps it was because I didn't have anyone else to turn to? Although, that in itself was a reason to trust him less. He could have moved all the pieces on the board so that I was isolated and had no other option but to rely on him.

As if sensing my inner turmoil, Nixon entered his room at that moment, his deep brown eyes sweeping over me warily. "What's wrong? You look like you're on the verge of a panic attack."

My mouth opened and shut, no words forthcoming. I balled my trembling hands into fists. I couldn't let him know my suspicions, otherwise it would blow any advantage I might have. Plus, on the off chance I was wrong, I didn't want to insult him so he wouldn't help me find Austin. "I … well …" *Pull it together! You can do this*! "What got the idiot healer so riled up?"

Nixon expelled a long breath but ignored my question. "Get anything you need, we're heading out. There's a … situation."

My stomach twisted with a sense of foreboding. "What kind of situation?"

"A block of houses in a suburb near here … all of the families in them were found dead, murdered."

Shock vibrated through my limbs. "What?"

"Yeah, an entire street of families murdered. We need you to do your thing."

"O-Of c-course," I stammered, my skin heating with both anticipation and dread.

All those deaths … it would be horrific and … *delicious*. I shuddered at my dual reaction. Tracking down the killer was a priority, one I still found important, and yet my giddy anticipation warred for control, threatening to hinder my need to deliver justice.

Fuck. I'd been so focused on saving Austin, I kept forgetting, or denying, that it was probably too late for my own redemption.

Chapter 28

The ride to the site of the slayings/crime scene was a tense one. Nixon was suspiciously silent, as if he knew I was analyzing every little thing he did and was afraid to give his secrets away. But I wasn't to be deterred so easily. I mentally took note of every minute thing, even his song choices, in case he slipped up and unintentionally gave something away by way of the lyrics. My wariness had crossed the line into paranoia, but I simply couldn't take the chance of missing anything, no matter how seemingly insignificant. Not being able to read his emotions due to his void abilities made things all that much worse.

I can't take it anymore. I need to know if I can trust him or not, and I need to know now.

"Drop your shield and let me in your mind." The command tumbled from my mouth before I could think better of it, and I grimaced as I waited for the fallout of my verbal diarrhea.

Nixon glanced at me before returning his gaze to the road. "Why exactly? In all the years we were married, you never asked, not even once."

"That's because I didn't know you could voluntarily drop it, and you purposely let me believe you couldn't. You played along with my misconception so I wouldn't learn the truth … about Austin and my past." My nails dug into my palms. "I need to know—"

Fuck it. I'm over playing his games. Plus, he probably already knows why I want in his mind. He'd have to be an idiot not to at this point.

I stared at his tense profile a few seconds before saying, "I need to know if I can trust you or not."

Nixon's knuckles whitened as his grip tightened on the steering wheel. "Why the fuck wouldn't you be able to trust me?"

"Because you lied to me all those years."

"You know why I did. You had—"

"I don't give a fuck why you did it. None of your reasons changes the fact that you lied to me about my past and pretended to be someone to me that you weren't." I ground my teeth together and leaned closer to him. "Let me in your damn mind, Nixon."

His jaw muscles jumped before he spit out one single syllable. "No."

I blinked at him in disbelief. No? Just like that. No reason, no attempted excuse? Just … no. Whatever he had tucked away behind the privacy of his void shield had to be more damning than flat-out denying me. He had to know that his response was a big red flag, alerting me to the fact that I couldn't trust him. So if he was willing to risk that then …

Shit.

My mind was still reeling when Nixon guided the SUV smoothly into a suburban neighborhood. Eagerness washed over me as I reached out with my senses, hoping to get a read on things, but instead, I slammed right into Nixon's void wall. My lip curled as I fought to contain my anger. I would have to temporarily put aside my issues with Nixon until we weren't at a crime scene.

I sighed heavily. "Who's here?"

"FBI has already been called in. I'm just surprised they got here so fast," Nixon muttered before continuing in a louder voice meant for me. "They think we're a special branch that handles this kind of shit. Let me do the talking. Remember, we don't have Austin here to tinker around with anyone's minds. I was hoping to beat them here, but since we didn't, we're going to have to play along."

"You don't have to remind me that he's not here," I spat. "I'm well aware." But it was true that I probably needed to be reminded to be extra careful. When Nixon and I had actually worked for the US government, we had the proper credentials, and when we'd had a full team working under Natalie we hadn't needed them. Now was a different story.

Nixon pulled up behind several other black SUVs and turned off the engine. He slid out without another word, his shoulders tense. Reluctantly, I decided it was best if I did what he asked and let him take the lead. My nerves ratcheted up as I pondered how I was supposed to pick up on the death emotions without having an over-the-top reaction. I definitely wouldn't have an understanding audience, and there was no good way to explain my enjoyment amidst the horror we were sure to find.

I nibbled on my thumbnail as I watched Nixon flash his fake credentials. He waved me forward, and I did the same before, keeping my gaze carefully averted.

"How long have you been here?" Nixon asked one of the men.

"Not long, we're still doing preliminaries." He paused before continuing, "But I thought you guys already had a team sent over? They arrived before we did."

"Yes, we did, but I've brought Agent Bevans, and she specializes in this kind of thing. She was working another case, so it took her a bit longer to become available."

The agent grunted his acceptance before waving his hand to the right. "They're in the house next to this one if you want to catch up with them first."

"Of course," Nixon said and began walking across the yard.

I scurried after him, whispering as soon as we were out of earshot, "What the hell is going on? I thought it was just us?"

"It is."

"Then who the hell—" *Austin! Of course! It has to be him.* But my excitement quickly fizzled as I realized the full scope of the situation. What if all the deaths had been carried out for Austin's benefit to feel them? Or worse, what if he'd finally fallen off the cliff and was now participating in murders for his own enjoyment? My heart squeezed as my chest tightened painfully.

"Sam …" Nixon rested his hand gently on my shoulder. "Calm down. Do you really think Austin is going to let us catch up to him so easily?"

Biting my tongue, I stared up into Nixon's fathomless brown eyes. *Why am I so paranoid all of a sudden? Nixon could have easily, and justifiably according to most, had Austin killed with the supposed evidence against him. And yet Nixon had held back and let me follow my hunch. Regardless of how much Nixon wants me, and the despicable things he's done to have me, he would always have my six. And despite his open disgust of Austin, he continued to help me even if he does voice his objections frequently. He's a good man. Trustworthy.*

Nixon released me and turned to enter the house, and I reluctantly trailed along behind him, not knowing what to expect. Even though I was eager to feel death emotions, I wasn't thrilled about the potential gruesome scenes that potentially awaited us. Especially if children were involved.

As it turned out, I didn't need to worry about any of it since the house was completely and utterly devoid of any kind of remnants of life. No bodies, no agents, not even a pet goldfish. The entire space was empty save the furnishings. Confusion nettled. Why exactly would the agents we just talked to direct us to a nonexistent crime scene? None of it made sense.

Something's obviously wrong. I eyed Nixon warily. "What the hell is going on?"

Nixon shook his head slowly, sharing my confusion. "Damned if I know."

Before I could question him further, he was already marching back the way we came. I sprinted to keep up with his longer strides.

As we spilled out into the front yard, we were greeted with more of the unexpected. The FBI agents and their vehicles were gone, leaving no traces behind, as if they'd vanished into thin air.

"What the fuck?" Nixon muttered, swinging his gaze around.

Clutching at his forearm, I dug my nails into his flesh, my heart picking up speed. "Cal. It was Cal. He can put images in your mind or cause mirages. I'm not sure which, but he made me see Malcolm before …"

The memory of Cal convincing me that I was witnessing Malcolm kill one of my captors only to realize that I'd done it myself skittered across my brain. Cal had mind fucked us both this time.

Several dark SUVs skidded to a stop behind our vehicle, men, and a few women, hastily jumping out with weapons drawn.

"FBI! Stop where you are!" one of the real agents called from his kneeling stance just outside his SUV.

The rest of the agents rushed us.

Nixon and I both raised our hands. "We're FBI, too. My badge is in my back pocket." Knowing how twitchy officers could be sometimes, Nixon didn't make a move to retrieve the badge himself but stood perfectly still as one of the agents approached him while being heavily covered by his peers.

"Drop your shield," I hissed under my breath. "I might be able to get something on Cal if he isn't already gone." And Austin. I knew he'd been present as well. I could feel it with every fiber of my being. But I kept his name to myself since I knew mentioning him would only serve to slow Nixon down.

The instant Nixon's void shield dropped, my head swam, dizziness assaulting me. *So much death.* So much pain, but amidst all of it was exactly what I knew I would find ... *Austin.* The strength of his essence was staggering, the core of it imprinted on the scene to a level where it was like watching a movie in my mind. I'd never experienced anything like it before, and I wasn't exactly sure why I was now. I would question all of it later. For the moment, I simply let my eyes close so I could focus on observing the man I loved with a combination of yearning, love, and horror.

Cal's knuckles connected with a green door, and Austin stood slightly behind him, annoyance and anger dancing across his features. A smiling woman with olive skin and dark hair somewhere in her mid-thirties answered the door, opening it wider in silent invitation. Both Cal and Austin entered the house, Cal taking the lead. Trepidation quickly became Austin's primary emotion since he didn't know why he'd been brought to the home, although he knew it wouldn't end well no matter what the reason was.

Cal pulled out a 9mm handgun from a holster under his jacket and a large knife from a sheath at his back. He moved steadily through the house, killing everyone inside in an unhurried and yet efficient manner. Austin dropped to his knees just inside the front door, horrified, and yet of course, wanting—needing to feel the deaths. Despite his burning desire, he still fought, still struggled not to do what he craved more than anything in that moment.

His lips formed my name as he began to mumble it over and over, much like what I'd picked up on at the morgue. I realized he was attempting to stave off his dark cravings with thoughts of me. Unfortunately, it wasn't long before those thoughts went off the rails and arrived at the times when we'd been tied up in death emotions together. Those memories only served to worsen his predicament. He was like that—on his knees, trembling, and mumbling my name when Cal returned to the foyer covered in blood.

"This is fucking ridiculous," Cal snapped. "Why are you still trying to resist?"

Austin stopped mumbling my name and glared up at Cal. He hated that S.O.B. and wouldn't mind feeling his death.

"All right, get up," Cal commanded. "We're done here." A sense of relief washed over Austin until Cal's next words. "Time to go next door."

"No!" Austin growled. "You can't. They're innocent. A-And

the children." Austin's mind flashed on the confused and terrified emotions of the three-year-old boy that Cal had just murdered. "No more children."

Cal grinned down at him. "Well, that's up to you. If you would just kill one person with your own hands, just one under your own steam, then I'll let the rest go. Buuut ..." Cal dragged the word out for dramatic effect. "If you resist, then I'm going to kill everyone. Every. Last. Person."

Austin sagged.

"Which can you live with?"

"Neither. I can't. I just can't." Austin ground his teeth together and the muscles in his jaw ticked. He hadn't felt this powerless since he was a kid and Natalie and David were using me to get to him. It was the same now. He knew if he didn't at least somewhat cooperate, they'd hurt me. Bring me in to use against him again. Or even worse, bring me to work with him and he'd have no one to blame but himself for what happened to me. He had to protect me at all costs.

"Fine. I guess it's going to be the hard way with you, too. Your little wifey was almost as stubborn, but not as strong as you ... or, well, stronger in some respects and weaker in others." He snorted. "I guess the two of you really are a good match. It kind of makes me want to throw up."

Cal pushed past Austin who remained on his knees in the foyer, and went to the next house. Austin felt it all. All the beautiful death emotions seeping into his system, making him buzz with life and yet filled with the guilt that they were all dying because of him. But he couldn't—he just couldn't kill someone in cold blood. At least not someone innocent. All the dying emotions tore at him and rebuilt him, over and over again. He yanked at his hair while he clenched his jaw to the point of pain.

"Sam, my Sammy—fuuuuck. I need you and I can't have you. I can't, I just can't." Austin was struggling with his wants, his needs, his own sense of self. And last, but not least, he was struggling to control his abilities, something he hadn't had to deal with in a very long time, maybe over a decade.

Even though what I was picking up on was only residue attached to the scene because of the strong death emotions, it felt raw and visceral, the pain coursing through Austin reaching into my chest and ripping it apart piece by piece. It was my fault. I'd done that to him—caused him the agony of having to face down the silent marauder I'd let in the back door. And it was like I'd abandoned him to fight alone.

Austin crumpled to the floor, a soul-shattering wail erupting from the depths of his chest. He was losing the battle—losing himself under the weight of feeling all that death.

Then things began to shift.

First, it was evident in his features, they morphed from anguish to serenity in a matter of seconds. Then his shoulders relaxed, and his hands dropped away from his hair. His eyes snapped open, blazing with something I couldn't quite get a sense of, his gaze glittering with it. And as that dark gaze seemingly peered through me, realization hit.

The Austin I knew and loved was gone.

He stood slowly, assessing his surroundings with a cold detachment even as his lips curled up at the corners slightly.

Nixon's void shield slammed down, yanking me back

to the present. "Nooo!" I screamed as I dropped to my knees and curled into myself.

He can't be. He isn't. He's not really gone. He's just lost. Yes. He's just lost and I'm going to have to fight harder to find him—save him. But I can do it. I will do it. Because I love him with everything that I am. Love like that can't be for nothing. It has to mean something. I will never abandon him even if I have to follow him to the depths of hell and drag him kicking and screaming out. Time ... I just need time to think. To sort out what I need to do.

Someone touched my shoulder, but my eyes were unfocused, my attention turned inward.

I barely registered Nixon's deep voice as he spoke to someone. "No. Back off. I shouldn't have brought her. She wasn't ready. All of this is too traumatic for her. There was an incident before ... yeah ... PTSD."

I wanted him gone, though. His void shield was in the way, and I needed to get another glimpse of Austin. I had to be sure I didn't miss something. Did he kill any of the other people with his own hands? And did he still think he'd erased himself from my memory? I had so little information and even the tiniest detail could make all the difference in the end ...

"Come on, Sam. We're going to get you home." Strong hands helped me to my feet, and I allowed myself to be blindly led away.

I need to think, I just need to think ...

Chapter 29

NIXON

Years of lying. One lie always spilled into the next, and just when I thought I'd figured a way past the web of deceit, all my plans fell apart. Nothing was happening the way it was supposed to. My mistake was that I'd counted too much on other people, but what choice did I have if I wanted to keep my secrets hidden from Sam? I'd considered the possibility of certain things going wrong, but not to this level. It'd become apparent that Cal was playing both sides when I found out what he'd done when he took her.

I'd been played for a fool, the notion enraging and humbling.

I thought I'd taken everything into consideration, every possibility carefully planned for. That's why I'd made the deal with Natalie to take temporary control of her agency if she agreed to disappear. From my position of power, I'd have immediate control, and I needed it. All I had to do was promise her that I would deliver Austin to David's old task force even though I wasn't sure why that bargain was still in place with David now being dead. But I didn't care in the end because she relented on me keeping Sam. If Natalie did what I wanted, I would do what she wanted.

Natalie gave me the evidence against Austin and various contacts that I could use if I needed them, such as Dr. Litzkin. She'd also given me the list of empaths so that I could track them down. She told me that she suspected experiments and old tactics for recruitment were still being done, but she'd obviously had no idea that some of them had been in contact with each other, or that someone would be a step ahead of us the entire time. She gave me everything to use as I saw fit, and I was doing a pretty damn good job until someone killed those two empaths in Pittsburgh for Sam to feel. That's when things really started going to shit.

That also raised the question … Did Natalie want our childhood memories returned to us? Too bad she didn't know I never lost mine. That's why I'd known Sam the moment I'd laid eyes on her. She was the girl that kept me alive when I was being tortured all those years ago. Natalie clearly had some ulterior motives of her own when it came to us, but none of it mattered now since things were completely FUBAR.

Natalie was in hiding with no way for me to contact her. She'd told me she would return in a few months with an explanation, but until then she'd be as good as dead.

Austin had been flipped, but I hadn't been able to free Sam from the bond with him first. Which meant everything I'd done was for nothing. And Cal? Fuck, my void shield didn't work when he was around. It was something he'd clearly kept hidden from me on purpose. He was supposed to take Sam hostage to give me a chance to work on Austin from my side. I was hoping to separate them without having to kill him, since part of the deal with Natalie was to hand him over to David's old team. But then Cal let Sam escape.

It was my fault, I'd been too cavalier with the information I had given Cal. I'd gotten too cocky, and I slipped up. I was already starting to rack up collateral damage, like with Taryn's death. I'd never trusted Cal completely, but I also hadn't considered the possibility that he would go against the plan, especially since Natalie was the one who suggested using him. She'd claimed he was trustworthy enough for the right price, and I'd paid him plenty.

I kept attempting to adjust my plans to take into consideration my vision of the future, but things were changing too fast and too drastically for me to get a decent read anymore—and that had me worried.

Whatever Sam had picked up on at the crime scene had her staring blankly out the window in a stupor. Obviously, it had to do with Austin, and my gut was telling me that he had crossed the line and was now like Malcolm. If that was truly the case, then how the hell was I going to get close enough to Austin to steal his powers?

Maybe I'd just have to kill Austin and Cal, and steal both of their abilities. After all, neither one of them knew I had such a talent … in fact, no one knew I could siphon off others' powers. Although it wouldn't be my secret for long. My end game was to do whatever needed to be done to make Sam mine.

Fuuuuck. I hit my fist on the steering wheel. I had so many fucking questions. I wasn't the only one playing games to get what they wanted. I couldn't trust anyone anymore. Except Sam …

I glanced at her still form as she continued to stare out the window at the quickly moving scenery. I could always trust Sam. The problem was getting her to trust me.

Chapter 30

My mind circled around and around, spiraling out of control, my eyes blinded to my surroundings. How could I possibly save Austin when I wasn't much better off than him? No matter what angle I looked at the problem from, I just couldn't seem to come up with any kind of viable solution or plan. The very real temptation of simply letting go—of giving up and letting myself have the things I truly craved was undeniable. It would be so easy to fall into the abyss of feeling death emotions with Austin. Nothing but us would matter. My thoughts drifted to a time when Austin had promised to protect me no matter what.

Austin's hands slid into my hair, and he pulled my head back so I could meet his gaze over the line of his body. "I'll never hurt you." His eyes bore into mine, fierce and protective. "And I'll kill anyone who tries."

"But what if I deserve to die?" I whispered.

"No, you listen to me right now. There's nothing more important to me than you. Fuck everything else. I don't care anymore. If you needed to kill someone every day for the rest of your long life to survive, God fucking help me, I'd bring you your victim every time, if that's what it took. I love you unconditionally and I won't let anyone take you away from me again. Knowing what it feels like to think you were gone forever ... it changed everything."

A single tear escaped my eye, sliding down my cheek. "I love you."

I knew Austin meant what he'd said. He would do anything to protect me. Would it be wrong for me to do the same? I simply wanted to be with the man I loved. Perhaps we were meant to be tainted by death. What if it was our destiny and I was wasting time without him when I didn't need to? Sure, if I had a choice, I'd prefer to be with him and not have us both crave death. But, in the end, no one was perfect, least of all Austin and me. Did our flaws translate to us not being able to enjoy our love?

I was torn. Every time I came to what I thought was a definitive decision, I ultimately wavered. I claimed that I was going to follow through on a plan only to be swept off course by me questioning my own motives. As an empath, it was natural to be run by my emotions, which led to a bit of indecisiveness periodically since emotions could change on a dime. But lately, I was focusing on all the wrong things, and I'd lost control completely.

"Sam, we're here," Nixon said.

I didn't respond. I simply lacked the energy to bother with Nixon and the concern emanating from him.

After a few beats of silence, he made his way around to the passenger door and scooped me into his arms. I slumped limply against him, my eyes fluttering shut.

What do I do? How do I save him? And do I really need to? Maybe I should just go to him? But if I do that .... I don't want to kill people. I'm not sure I could be happy if I became that kind of monster. So what do I do ... what do I do? Fuck. What the hell do I do?

At some point, I slipped into a fitful sleep.

"Sam, my good Sammy girl." Austin's voice wound around and through me, caressing my senses with its loving embrace. *"I need you. I don't want to be separated from you anymore."*

"Austin?" My eyes snapped open, and I floundered to figure out where I was. My hand smacked into a lamp, and I fumbled to switch it on, blinking against the sudden blaze of light. But the small room was empty, no Austin in sight. Confusion nettled for a moment before I realized he was speaking to me in my mind. "Austin," I breathed. "Where are you? I'll come and get you. I can save you—"

"I don't need saving, Sam. And neither do you. We were wrong about everything." His voice was as smooth as silk, and I shivered involuntarily.

Apprehension twisted my gut, pushing bile into my esophagus. "*Everything* is kind of vague. What were we wrong about specifically?"

"We shouldn't have to fight what we are. We began traveling

down this road the minute you walked into my room in the hospital that day when we were kids. We're not like other people, we see and feel things others never will, and with the light comes the dark. We are the dark. We should stop pretending we're something we aren't—and never will be."

My heart took off at a gallop. "What are you saying?"

"Come to me. We'll enjoy it all together and we'll protect each other, just like we promised. I'll never let anything happen to you. I love you. That could never change."

I can't let that happen. I just ... can't. No matter how much I want to accept it. "No, Austin, you don't know what you're saying."

"I know exactly what I'm saying. Remember how it was after the blast? How good it was between us? How close we felt to each other? We could have that until the day we died. It could always be like that. Don't you want it?"

"I do want it, so fucking much. But I don't want to be a killer. I can't become that. Austin, please. Let me help you."

His irritation pushed at me. *"What's the difference between what we do on Natalie's task force and what we'd do here? We've killed people, Sam. No matter what way you look at it, that's what we do—we kill people. We might as well be together and enjoy it. I want my wife with me. We took vows, Sam."*

"I don't—"

"I guess you need a little push."

I frowned, not liking the new direction of our conversation. "A little push?"

"Trust me."

"I do. You know I do, but—"

Austin shoved into my mind and stole the reins from me. Suddenly, I was a prisoner within my own body. I was still in touch with all of my senses, but Austin was pulling my strings like I was a human puppet.

I fought him, but his control was complete, and I watched numbly as my hand fumbled for the door. *"Stop!"* I hissed. "Austin. Please. Why are you doing this?"

"Trust me," he repeated.

My body stumbled down the hallway and continued until it came to the west wing living quarters. I then entered one of the rooms. It was dark and silent inside, and Austin made me creep in quietly. I was forced to stop at the side of a bed, and I could just make out someone asleep on it in the dim lighting. Fear cinched my chest. *"What are you doing?"*

"Not what I'm doing, what you're doing. You're going to kill her."

"No! Austin, please. Don't do this. Please."

He didn't respond, and I watched in horror as my hands picked up a pillow that had been knocked to the floor, and pressed it over the face of whoever was in the bed.

"It's Tasha," Austin supplied. *"The blonde healer that you can't stand. I thought you might enjoy this one a bit more than the other options."*

"I don't like her, but I don't want to kill her."

"Please. I know you, Sam. She tried to seduce me. She

stripped off all her clothes and told me I could do anything I wanted to her." He chuckled. *"How does that make you feel?"*

Jealousy and anger burned through my veins. *"I won't deny that I want to smash her face in, but that doesn't translate to me actually wanting to murder her."* I ground my teeth together as I imagined my fist connecting with her pert nose.

"Sam." Austin clicked his tongue. *"You forget, I can see into all of the darkest parts of your mind and set them free—you're already killing her."*

My gaze locked onto my hands as they pressed the pillow over Tasha's face. Bile burned my throat and mouth. She was now awake and struggling fruitlessly against me. I wasn't physically stronger than her, but I had risen up on the bed and was using my entire body as leverage to hold her down so I could suffocate her.

"Now, how about we just slip in and enjoy her death together, as husband and wife?"

It was as if Austin was physically there with me, standing behind me, his hard chest pressed into my back as he helped me hold the pillow over Tasha. I shuddered as he pulled us both into her mind, surrounding us with her death emotions.

It was a perfect mix of shock and denial which couldn't have been any sweeter. Tasha thought she was safe at the compound, and her security fed the denial even as she registered her life slipping away. Her lungs burned from lack of oxygen and her legs had begun to twitch involuntarily. It would all be over soon, a vibrant life cut short by the heavy hand of death.

The usual euphoria rushed through me, only enhanced by Austin's, but something was different this time ... there was no slow burn of guilt afterwards, and without it, a missing piece clicked into place, altering me irrevocably.

I collapsed to the floor, fully enraptured. *"I want you inside me,"* I purred at Austin.

"Yeah, baby, I want that, too. But you have to come to me." Austin's voice was like liquid sex, cascading down my body with promises of pleasure. *"I'm waiting for you my good Sammy girl. I'm waiting—"*

Austin was ripped from me abruptly, and I jolted up, blinking dazedly. Nixon's silhouette filled the doorway, his hand hovering over the light switch. "Sam, no," he rasped. "What did you do?"

"I-I ..." Without my connection to Austin, things felt different, and I was unsure. Glancing up at the bed, my gaze locked onto Tasha's limp arm hanging over the edge.

My muscles seized. "Oh God. I killed her. I-I killed her. And I enjoyed it. We enjoyed it."

Nixon's eyes darkened as he seemed to come to a decision. He crossed the room in a few strides and scooped me up in his arms. I squirmed within his grasp, fear for what he would do making it hard to breathe.

"Nixon, please. I didn't mean to. I didn't have control ..." I swallowed the rest of my words. I refused to throw Austin under the bus. But would Austin blame me if it saved my life? Would he—

"Stop." Nixon shook me harshly. "After everything, do you actually believe I would hurt you?" His upper lip curled. "I need to get you out of here, fast. I'm done pretending like any of these places are safe for you anymore. I'm taking you as far away from everything as I possibly can before it's too late. And one day, eventually, you'll thank me for it."

I stared at the hard lines of his face as realization sunk in. *No. He's not stealing me from Austin again.* Biting his neck viciously, I forced Nixon to lose his grip on me and I plunged to the floor, landing in a heap. I scrambled to my feet, beginning a mad dash down the hallway away from my wannabe captor.

Nixon tackled me to the ground, and I let out a screech, the coppery tang of blood running down the back of my throat. Gasping for air, I bucked and twisted, trying to dislodge him from my back. Something sharp jabbed into my right shoulder, spreading liquid fire through my veins.

My lips went numb, and my eyelids drooped. *What the fuck? Does he just carry syringes with drugs in them to knock people out at a moment's notice or—*

Everything went dark.

Acknowledgments

As an overthinker, acknowledgments are quite an arduous task for me. I wonder if I'm being lackluster or too intense with the thanks. Or did I forget someone? Possibly I gave too much credit to someone and therefore slighted someone else who actually did a ton. A part of me doesn't want to include these in my books at all because the people I appreciate should know it already … or do they??? No matter how I look at it these damn acknowledgments make me friggin' sweat.

But here they are anyways since if I don't include them then people will probably think I'm ungrateful and weird. I mean, I am weird, but I don't want people to think that. I am grateful though, so I'll just go-ahead and make this uncomfortable for everyone. Heh.

Okay, here I go. Right now. Actual acknowledgments to follow. Hopefully, they represent an appropriate level of gratitude to all the people in my life that deserve it.

(And yep … I have totally copy & pasted what comes next from my *Replayed* book acknowledgments, which I originally took from *Virtual Reality Bites* acknowledgments. I thought maybe after *Replayed* that I'd come up with something better. Or at least something new. Obviously not. So this is now copy & paste edition #6. Or 7? 8? Who even knows anymore. Therefore, I'm thinking you should probably get used to it.)

My amazing Hubby! Words can't begin to explain how supportive and truly amazing he is. Hmmm … I think I already used the word amazing. But unlike in books, when honestly applied to someone, the word amazing means something, well, amazing. And my hubby is all of the things that word implies. Romance heroes are nothing compared to him.

Lindsay Tiry … what would I do without you? I hope I never have to find out. From cover design to interior graphics to logos, you do it all. Your talent is awe-inspiring, and I hope one day everyone else will be able to appreciate how you shine.

Melissa Ringsted … my illustrious editor. Without you, this book probably would have gone straight into the trash. Thank you for giving me the confidence to publish when I convinced myself that I was the worst writer in the history of writers, and for fixing all the words.

Ren, Kristin, Shona, Ruty … my O.G. chicas … I wouldn't be here without you. I'm beyond lucky to know all of you.

And last, but certainly not least, thank you to everyone who has taken the time to read this book. Hopefully, you enjoyed it, but even if you didn't, I still appreciate the fact that with so many options out there today, you even gave my book a fleeting chance.

About the Author

Ava Wixx escaped into books at a young age and decided to stay there. It was only a matter of time before she was driven to create her own fantasy worlds from fear of running out of places to explore.

Reader, writer, dreamer … Ava only toils in reality when absolutely necessary. She lives in North Carolina with her husband, and spoiled mini-poodle.

www.ingramcontent.com/pod-product-compliance
Lightning Source LLC
LaVergne TN
LVHW041113080826
845145LV00007B/1801

* 9 7 8 1 9 5 5 9 5 0 3 0 5 *